THE SCREAM
OF AN EAGLE

MARCUS LYNN DEAN

First published in 2019

Copyright © Marcus Lynn Dean 2019

MarcusLynnDean@gmail.com

For Karen
The love of my life.

Contents

Somewhere high overhead, the chilling sound of an eagle's scream pierces the quiet stillness of the Colorado morning. The Eagle; of all creatures, the one most loved by the Great Spirit. The eagle teaches the story of life. The man remembers first hearing the legend of the eagle when he was very young. From the veranda where he sits, he can't see the eagle. It is shielded from view by the overhang of the roof. From his vantage point, he sees only a couple of turkey buzzards circling just above the horizon to the northeast. He watches as the buzzards glide down toward the earth. A thought occurs to the man – *the story of life always ends in death*.

Chapter 1

There was, of course, nothing that the Federal Reserve could do to stop the collapse at that point. Just as there was nothing that the IMF or the rest of the world's central banks could do. They had already done way too much. The "quantitative easing" and debt burdens that had prevented the world's economies from going over the cliff in 2008 had served mainly to astronomically increase the height of that cliff. The climb to the top of that economic peak was decades in the making. The fall, once the economy went over the edge, was a precipitous drop; wiping out those decades of economic gains in just a few short weeks. Fortunately for the world's bankers and elites, having long ago seen what was coming, plans were already in place to take advantage of the crisis.

Robert Mendez sat in the same chair at the same large desk in the same office that he had occupied for the last seven years. The office was on the top floor of a major bank building in downtown Denver. The sign on his office door read Robert James Mendez – Senior VP. He had been promoted to Senior Vice President in charge of the investment division seven years ago, nearly to the day. Under Robert's investment guidance the bank's value, and the shareholders net worth, as well as his own, had grown astronomically. Now, all but the wealthiest and most powerful of those shareholders, and all of the common people who had deposits in the bank were pretty much losing everything.

The three large computer displays on Robert's desk looked almost the same as they had for his entire tenure here. There were, however, some striking differences. The series of ticker tapes still scrolled continuously across the screen on the left, but instead of a series of stock and market listings and numbers, each ticker continuously displayed the same message; **MARKETS CLOSED.** All of the world's financial markets had been forced to close. The world's economic systems were totally frozen.

The central screen showed the same email inbox that it always had. The only difference was the incredible number of unread email messages sitting in wait.

The third screen, the one on the right, was the one that had captured Robert's attention.

The third screen was the one with his favorite newsfeed. He had the volume muted but sat spellbound by the images on the screen. They were mostly a series of views from cities all over the United States, as well as most of the rest of the world. Views of riots in the streets, the rioters anger focused on governments and banks all over the world. Banks that had been locked down, the flow of money shut down completely, as governments and central bankers tried to figure out what to do now. As bank depositors rioted to get their money out of the banks, Robert sat there and knew that the money the depositors thought they had securely stashed away was an illusion. The money had always been, in reality, just an illusion. The world's governments and central banks, the Federal Reserve of the United States and the IMF had, over time, created the world's largest Ponzi scheme; and now, that Ponzi scheme was unraveling and there was nothing anyone could do to stop it. Robert, along with the rest of the world, was now just a witness to the greatest economic disaster of all time. A disaster that would, in later years, come to be known simply as "The Catastrophe".

He decided that it might be best to just go home. Not that there was any chance of rioters being able to breach the bank's security, but there was nothing he could do at this point to change a thing. *No, nothing to be done now,* he thought. It would be a few days before he would need to be back at his desk. It would take a little time for the Federal Reserve and the International Monetary Fund to implement their long-planned policies. If the rabble was protesting now, wait until they saw what came next. Oh, they'd be able to get some of their money out of the banks, but there would be a catch. Most people would be demanding cash, and cash they would get, in strictly limited quantities, of course. But they'd get something else along with the cash they withdrew, they'd get a brand-new tax; a tax on cash.

Most people hadn't given much thought to the tiny magnetic strip that had been placed in bills over the past few decades. They had no idea how that little strip would be used to, once again, force them to "bail out" the "big banks". Robert Mendez knew. Relatively simple really, charge interest on deposits, and let them take the cash out to avoid that interest. Then, when they spend that cash, that tiny little magnetic strip in the bills electronically takes a percentage of the transaction. A truly amazing construct – a tax on cash. A tax that, just like previous bailouts, goes back to where wealth truly belongs, in the hands of the elite few who rule the world's economies and, by extension, the world's governments. Robert may not have been in the very upper echelon of that elite group yet, but he had his plans. He knew his stock in the bank would have to become forfeit, and that it would have to appear that upper bank management had lost a great deal of wealth. He also knew that appearances of loss can be very deceiving.

He took one more look at the three screens on his desk before shutting them down. The elevator that was just across the hall from his office door took him directly to the second level of underground parking. He threw his briefcase into the back seat of the Cadillac SUV, slowly drove up the ramp that came out in the alley behind the bank, and headed home to

Chapter 2

Summertime at last! He had been anticipating spending some time out at his Grandpa's ranch since school started ten months ago. At twelve years old, it wasn't that he didn't have friends and playmates, but they just couldn't compete with the Blue River Ranch on the western slope near Kremmling. He wouldn't admit it to anyone, but he was especially looking forward to spending time with Anna.

"James, you have to promise me that you will do whatever Grandpa asks. I still don't feel very good about sending you out there by yourself." James smiled at the worried look on his mother's face.

"I'll be fine, Mom. Maybe you and Dad can drive out and pick me up, so I don't have to ride the train back."

Noni Mendez smiled at her son. It had been five years since the Catastrophe, and the world seemed to be getting somewhat back to normal. Public transportation was probably as safe as it had ever been, and she knew that somewhere in the crowd of people getting on the train, there would be at least one member of the Mendez security team. Someone whose sole purpose in being on the train was to keep Robert Mendez' heir safe. It had been Robert's idea to let James experience travel with the masses. Noni wasn't really worried about her son's safety. What really bothered her, more than letting James go to Kremmling by himself, was a longing to go with him. A longing to return to her childhood home.

"I know you'll be fine, James," she tried to hide her longing from her son. "It's your Grandpa I'm worried about. He's not getting any younger, you know. You just make sure you help him every way you can."

Grandpa Chuck didn't seem old at all to James. In a lot of ways, Grandpa Chuck seemed to be in better shape than his dad. Of course, it was probably easier to stay in shape as a rancher than it was sitting behind a desk on the top floor of an office in Denver, even if the office had its own private gym.

"Grandpa's not old, he can probably still ride circles around most anybody else on the ranch."

He's probably right, she thought. *Dad probably can still ride circles around most anybody.* She grabbed James by both shoulders, amazed once again that her little boy was nearly as tall as she was. And his shoulders seemed so broad and strong.

"I know you're right James, I just worry about him more since your Grandma died. Wish he didn't have to be all alone on that great big ranch."

James put his arms around his mother and hugged her.

"You know, Mom, he's not really alone. He has the whole Duran family living just down the lane in the old house. You just wish we could live there too, instead of here."

Noni hugged her only son. *He knows me too well*, she thought, as tears formed in her dark brown eyes. *I told myself I wouldn't cry.*

The train ride from Denver to the small town of Kremmling, Colorado was long and slow. At times it seemed like he could have made better time walking.

It was one of the combo trains that had been put together in the years after the Catastrophe. With most people no longer able to afford the costs of personal transportation, the quickest solution to transport problems was to add some passenger cars to freight trains to better facilitate mass transit. This particular train had both; one of the old Amtrak cars, and one of the new people mover cars that had been designed to carry more people on shorter trips. It also had ninety-eight freight cars, at least twenty of which were empty coal cars, and thirty loaded fuel cars; as well as the usual thirty or forty blue tanker cars that carried water to the parched west. The whole thing was pulled and pushed over the mountains by three diesel-powered locomotives in the front and two in the rear. All along the way, there were signs of the construction projects that were running power lines along the tracks. Power lines that would, someday, enable the replacement of the diesel locomotives with electrics.

James was lucky enough to get one of the window seats in the new people mover car, where he could watch the scenery slowly passing by. At the moment, the scenery was at a standstill as the train sat on one of the sidings, waiting for another train coming from the west to pass. The only things making much progress were the water in the river and the trucks and a few cars on the old highway across the canyon from the parked train. James had seen this canyon from the other side a few times in his young life, as he and his mother had traveled along highway 40 back and forth from Denver to Kremmling. Most times when they traveled by car, they used I-70 through the old tunnels instead of driving over Berthoud Pass. As he thought about those trips, he realized that he could only recall his father accompanying them once. That was when his grandmother had died. He was very young at the time. The trips by car were always much faster than this trip by train, even though, to James, it always seemed to take forever. James remembered seeing trains on this side of the canyon from Highway 40 on the other side of the river, but this was the first time he had ever seen old Highway 40 from this vantage point.

"Still seems odd to see so little traffic on the old highway," the older man seated next to James said. "Of course, you're probably too young to remember what it was like before; before the Catastrophe that is."

James had been mostly trying to ignore the man, but the man was one of those people who can't help but talk to people, whether they're being ignored or not. James actually could remember when, what everyone now called the Catastrophe, had happened, but he didn't have many memories of the way things were before. He had only been seven years old when his dad came home from the bank, locked the big iron gates at the entrance to their driveway and told him not to dare leave the premises.

"When I was your age," the man continued, "that highway was filled with vehicles of all kinds. It was bumper to bumper traffic, especially on weekends. Now look at it, a few of the autonomous freight haulers and even fewer cars. Only rich folk can afford to travel by car anymore. Normal people can't even afford fuel for their old clunkers, let alone the price of a new EV.

James couldn't help but notice the contempt in the man's voice, especially when he spoke of "rich folk." He hadn't given too much thought to it before, but he knew that his family was included in the "rich folk" that the man spoke of. After all, the Mendez family always traveled by car. Robert Mendez had just recently made his yearly purchase of a brand-new Cadillac. It was totally electric, but what impressed James the most was the seating arrangement. It had two seats in front and two seats in the rear facing each other with a sort of console table in the middle. The two doors, one on each side between the seats, were nearly all glass, offering all four passengers fantastic views of whatever scenery was passing by. No one actually drove the car; the computer that was built into the center console "drove" the car. James wished he was in that car now, speeding along that old highway on the other side of the river.

"How long do we have to sit here?" James asked the man who had spoken to him.

"Not much longer now." The man replied, just as the east-bound train started flashing by the window on the other side of the train. "Where you headed, anyway?"

James felt a little bit uneasy about telling the stranger much, so he just said, "Kremmling," and turned back to the window.

"Kremmling, huh, that's my next stop as well. Bud Johnson," the man said, thrusting his hand out to shake.

James could see the extended hand from the corner of his eye, so he turned toward the man and shook hands. "James Mendez," he said, "I'm going to visit my grandpa." He didn't really know what else to say, so that was it.

"Business trip for me," Bud Johnson was a salesman. That was obvious even to a twelve-year-old boy. "I'm with Pro Foods, meeting with some of the ranchers out there."

James, like most people, had never heard of Pro Foods, but he did catch the part about meeting with ranchers. "My Grandpa's a rancher," he said. "His name's Chuck Pierson."

"What a coincidence, your Grandpa's one of the ranchers I want to meet with. Pro Foods wants to buy all your Grandpa's cattle. We're going to revolutionize the way America eats."

The big old 2019 Ford dually truck was the only vehicle James had ever known his Grandpa to drive. As they dodged the potholes in Highway 9, James wondered why Grandpa Chuck didn't get one of the new autonomous vehicles, maybe even electric instead of diesel.

"Grandpa how come you still drive this same old truck?" he asked. He didn't think his grandpa was poor. He wasn't like so many of the people back on the eastern slope who couldn't afford to own or drive a personal vehicle at all.

"Well James, I bought this truck new back in 2018 when we had a president who was making America great again. At the time, I really believed we were on the road to great things. Guess it's just a reminder of better times. Besides, being a rancher, I get enough fuel subsidy to help pay for the high cost of diesel.

Besides that, I don't much like electric vehicles. Suppose I'm just old fashioned."

It was about a twenty-mile drive south on Highway 9 from Kremmling to the confluence of Spider Creek and the Blue River, where the Blue River Ranch was located. On that drive, Chuck and James only met one other vehicle. James noticed that it was also an old beat up looking ranch truck, and Chuck waved at the driver as they met.

"Wonder why John's headed to town?" He muttered, as much to himself as to James. The ranchers who lived sparsely scattered out through this part of the country didn't make the trip to Kremmling very often. Chuck, himself, tried to limit the trip to about once a month. *Probably just needs to stock up*, he thought to himself. *Hope he can find what he needs, shortages are definitely getting to be more common than they used to be.*

"Have you got a horse ready for me to ride?" James' question interrupted his grandpa's thoughts. "Does Anna know I'm coming?" He was getting more excited as they got closer to the ranch.

"Whoa, I thought you came out here to see me, not Anna". Chuck teased. "As for a horse, I have a surprise for you this year. I'm going to let you pick your own out of the herd. If you can catch it and ride it, I'll give it to you for your birthday."

James blushed slightly at the tease about Anna and then frowned. "Dad won't let me have a horse, Grandpa. You know that," he said.

Chuck smiled. "Guess it'll just have to be our little secret. Your horse can live here on the ranch and it'll be yours whenever you're here. Your dad doesn't even need to know." Then the thought occurred to the old rancher that it might be fun if Robert Mendez did know about the horse, just to piss him off.

James was watching anxiously as they drove up the lane to the Blue River Ranch headquarters, but there was no sign of anyone, let alone Anna. Chuck pulled the big Ford truck into the metal shop building near the big house.

"Where is everyone?" James asked.

"The Durans are all helping get the herd up to the high country. Had to trail them up this year, diesel's too expensive to haul 'em. All but Shelly, that is. I bet she's in the house getting dinner ready. You looking for Anna?" Chuck teased, knowing that was the case.

"Ralph and Cody and Anna all got to help move the herd?" James asked, careful to put Ralph and Cody, Anna's younger brothers, ahead of her. "Wish I'd got here sooner, so I could help, too." Trailing the herd seemed like a great adventure to James.

"They've been out for three days. Should be home this evening. It's a long ride up to Elk Park and back. Think you're up to three full days in the saddle?"

"Sure – I love riding." James was as certain as he sounded, the inexperience and optimism of youth blinding him to the rigors of three long days on horseback.

It was almost dusk when James heard the sound of hooves on the graveled lane behind the big house. He'd been sitting on the front porch; Grandpa Chuck was inside. He jumped up and ran to the corner of the house to meet them. Anna was in the lead riding Pintada, her black and white paint, followed by her brothers, Ralph and Cody. The two boys were riding side by side, and Clyde Duran, the longtime ranch foreman, was bringing up the rear. Clyde was leading three pack horses in a line behind him. The pack saddles were all but empty. They'd been used to haul supplies for the two cowboys that would spend the summer with the herd up in the high country. Someone, normally Clyde, would be making that trek with fresh supplies every couple of weeks for the rest of the summer. It would only be a two-day ride, now that the herd was already up there, and James had the thought that maybe he could go next time.

In spite of the dust and grime of the trail, Anna was a beautiful young girl. She had dark skin, long black hair, and eyes that were an even deeper brown than James'. Her face lit up in a radiant smile when she saw James come around the corner of the house. She reined up and dismounted when she got to James. She felt like hugging him, but she knew that would never do. Especially not in front of her dad and her brothers.

"Hi James," was all she could manage to say, as she stood there holding the end of the reins in both hands in front of her. Even that brought a little blush to her face. The blush deepened a little more as she realized she was covered with trail dust and must look a mess.

James couldn't help but think that she looked just like an Indian princess, even though she was dressed head to toe in western cowgirl clothes. From the western style straw hat on her head to the chaps on her legs and the boots on her feet, she was covered with dust from the trail. Anna had definitely changed since he last saw her two years ago. Her face had begun to lose some of the roundness of childhood, and the high cheekbones of her Native American heritage were more pronounced, but what James really noticed were her breasts. She hadn't had breasts when he had last seen her. Now, the youthful mounds were all too obvious underneath her dusty denim shirt. It was his turn to be embarrassed, as he realized he had been staring at her breasts. He looked up into her dark brown eyes.

"Hi Anna," it was as if neither one of them knew what to say.

Fortunately, Ralph and Cody came to the rescue greeting James and asking when he'd arrived, and what he had been up to. Then Clyde Duran pulled up the Buckskin he was riding. Clyde was not as big a man as James' grandfather; he was about six feet tall and probably weighed around a hundred eighty, but he had an imposing presence about him that had a way of making James feel slightly uneasy.

"Yo James," his deep voice didn't help with James' feeling of unease. "Good to see you again."

"Good to see you too, sir – I mean Clyde," James stammered, remembering that Clyde didn't like being called sir.

Clyde swung down off his horse with a groan and stuck his big right hand out to James to shake. "How's your mother?" he asked James as they shook hands.

"She's fine," he answered. He couldn't help but notice that Clyde hadn't asked about his family, or his mom and dad; only about his mother.

"Good to hear," Clyde said to James. Then, to the group, "let's get these horses put away. Come on James, you can help."

Walking side by side with Anna, as she led Pintada to the barn, made the long train trip all worth it. *I get to spend a whole month here*, James thought. At that moment, to his twelve-year-old mind, a month might just as well have been an eternity.

James, Anna, Ralph, and Cody had been playing in the willows that lined the banks of Spider Creek. The willows were so thick that you had to follow the trails and openings made by animals, mostly cows, to get through them. The trails meandered and worked their way through the willows from opening to opening in such a crooked winding manner that the effect was that of a maze, with trails crisscrossing each other and going every which way. The kids, mainly the Duran siblings, since James was only there occasionally, had made various play forts and hideouts from cut willows and scraps of wood, tin, and whatever else they could find. They spent hours on end playing in the willows. It was their own private playground.

James had been at the ranch for three full days now, and he and Anna were both getting tired of the younger boys always being around. James was finding more and more that he wanted to be alone with Anna, instead of having Ralph and Cody tagging along everywhere they went. He seemed to have two main desires. One was to catch and claim one of the horses in the south pasture, the other was to spend time with Anna – alone, just the two of them. So far, he had been unable to satisfy either desire, and he had less than a month before he would have to go back to Castle Pines.

"Let's play hide and seek," James said.

Ralph and Cody were all for it. Without knowing what James had in mind, Anna thought it was too childish. Wondering why James was so intent on playing such a childish game, she finally relented, and after a few rounds of rock, paper, scissors, it was decided that Cody was first to be "it". He stood in one of the play forts, covered his eyes with his hands and began to count out loud to one hundred. Ralph immediately started sneaking down one of the trails toward the creek, moving as quietly as he could to prevent Cody from hearing which direction he had gone. James looked at Anna, put a finger to his lips for silence, and signaled her to follow him in the opposite direction, up a trail that led quickly out of the willows to the back of the log barn. Now Anna's curiosity was definitely piqued. *What is he up to?* she wondered, following behind as quietly as she could.

The log barn was one of the oldest buildings on the ranch. Constructed of logs cut from the surrounding countryside, it had been built so well more than a hundred years ago that it was not only still standing, it was structurally as sound as any of the newer ranch buildings. It was the original horse barn on the BR, with seven stalls and a tack room at ground level and a hayloft above. The hayloft was huge. It was probably twice as tall as the ground floor, with a large set of double doors on the front matching the sliding main entrance doors directly below. The log barn had been designed and built in the days when hay was stacked loose, not baled; the huge volume of space in the loft a requirement of stacking loose hay. There was a large semi-circular corral attached to the back of the log barn. It was actually not round but was constructed of two dozen twelve-foot sections arranged in a semi-circular shape with the back wall of the log barn forming the straight side of the corral. Each section was about eight feet tall, made of spruce and lodgepole pine rails stacked between two large cedar posts. There was another large single cedar post set in the center of the corral. The post in the center was worn totally smooth by the countless ropes that had been wrapped around it over the years, as a multitude of horses had been trained to ride.

"Where are we going?" Anna whispered, even though they were far enough away that they could no longer hear Cody counting.

"I'll show you," James said, as he quietly opened the gate leading into the round corral.

Closing the gate behind them as quietly as he had opened it, he led Anna through the open barn door. Just inside this back door to the barn, there was a ladder made of old rough cut two by fours nailed to the wall. The top edge of most of the boards was rounded and worn smooth by a hundred years of use. A few of the boards had been replaced by newer smooth cut two by fours. James could easily feel the difference between the old boards and the new ones. The top edges of the newer boards were still square and not nearly as smooth as the old ones. He quickly climbed the ladder which led up into the loft above. Anna followed close behind. The hayloft was familiar, both of them having been there many times before. It was mostly empty this time of year, the hay that had filled the cavernous space the previous fall had mostly been fed to the stock over the course of the long winter.

Sunlight shining through the open doors at the west end of the loft illuminated what was left of last year's hay crop. Just a few dozen bales still stacked in the southeast corner. These were the small rectangular hay bales of old. The Blue River ranch had never made the switch to the giant thousand-pound bales that had become so popular in the later years of the twentieth century. Chuck Pierson was somewhat of an enigma that way. He had embraced much of the new technology that had been developed over the course of his life but stubbornly refused to change many of the older ways of doing things.

James walked over and sat down on one of the hay bales, Anna followed and sat down on the bale next to him. James looked at her questioning gaze.

"Anna, do you have a boyfriend?" he asked, the question in a matter of fact way, much as if he'd asked her if she had a pet dog.

Anna wasn't sure how to respond. At eleven years old, with her body changing in ways she was constantly struggling to get used to, she had begun to occasionally find herself thinking about boys in ways she never had before. Whenever the thoughts of boy's bodies and the differences between men and women came to mind, she inevitably thought of James. She could feel herself blush.

"Do you want to be my boyfriend, James?"

By way of answer, James reached over and took her hand.

"Okay, you can be my girlfriend," he said. It wasn't his intention, but it sounded almost begrudging, as if he had resigned himself to the fact that he was going to have to put up with having a girlfriend. "It has to be our secret, though."

Anna smiled, James' touch, just holding hands, sent feelings through her young body that were totally new.

"Okay," she said. "It can be our secret, but James, if we are going to be boyfriend and girlfriend, we should kiss."

They leaned toward each other, not really knowing how to kiss in an adult manner. Turning their faces first one way, and then the other to avoid each other's noses, with closed mouths, their lips came together. James had kissed girls before, usually on a dare, or having lost a bet, but this was like nothing he had ever experienced. It was as if an electric current passed from Anna's lips through his, sending a tingling through his body and shutting out thought. He couldn't have said how long their lips touched. It could have been a split second, or it could have been an eternity.

"Allie allie outs in free, allie allie outs in free!" Cody's yells broke through the spell and the magic of the moment.

"Hurry," James said, breaking away from Anna. "Let's get back before they know where we are. This can be our secret place."

What secret? Anna thought as she followed James back down the ladder. *Everyone knows about the hayloft.*

James woke, startled that the sun was already streaming in the window. He had been dreaming, it took him a minute to realize where he was. In the dream, he'd been on a horse. He was riding bareback without a bridle or even a hackamore for control. The horse was taking him somewhere, his destiny totally under the control of the horse that seemed to be flying through clouds instead of running over the earth. They seemed to be trying to catch someone or some thing that was hidden beyond the cloudy mists. James had awakened just as he was about to glimpse whatever it was that was out there, ahead of them in the clouds.

His room at home, in Castle Pines, was on the west side of the house, but here in the room that was his at the Blue River Ranch, the window faced due east, and the morning sun shone through in all its glory. The smell of frying bacon focused his attention on the hunger that his growing body always awoke to. As he pulled on his jeans and boots, he thought about Anna. Yesterday he got a girlfriend, today he was going to catch himself a horse.

"Grandpa, do you ever eat anything besides bacon and eggs for breakfast?" James asked as he slid the last piece of bacon around on his plate.

"Well, I guess I am kind of a creature of habit," Chuck replied. "Sometimes I have steak and eggs, instead of bacon and eggs. You want me to fix steak and eggs tomorrow?"

"Do you have any cereal?" James asked, hopefully. "Or maybe some donuts or sweet rolls. We'll probably have steaks or burgers again for dinner."

"Well, maybe I can pick something up. I have to go to Kremmling again. The Department of Agriculture says I need to meet with that feller you told me about meeting on the train. You want to ride along?"

James felt instant disappointment. "Not really," he said. "I was hoping we could catch my horse today."

Chuck didn't miss the disappointment in his grandson's voice. "Tell you what, James, how 'bout you go over to the south pasture while I'm gone, and study the horses to see which one you want. Then, tomorrow, I'll help you catch the one you pick. I'd stay away from the big black, though, I'm not too sure about that one." Even as he said it, Chuck had an inward chuckle, thinking that now James wouldn't be able to resist picking Midnight, the big black three-year-old. The one that Chuck had already picked out to be James' horse.

"How can I get across the river?" James asked. The south pasture was on the other side of Spider Creek, and though the river wasn't very deep, there weren't enough stable rocks poking above the water to get across by stepping or leaping from rock to rock. James didn't relish the idea of wading across. "Can I use one of the old ATVs?" There were five old ATVs in the metal shop. They were covered with tarps that were in turn covered with dust.

"I doubt you could even get one started," Chuck answered, "we haven't used those old ATVs for years. The cost of gas got so high that we just went back to using horses. Maybe you could get Anna to saddle up her paint and take you across."

The brightening of James' demeanor at the thought of riding double with Anna wasn't lost on the old cowboy. *Ahh, to be a kid again*, he thought.

The south pasture wasn't a hay meadow but was about twenty acres of rolling hills that had been cleared of sagebrush and most trees over a century ago. Native dryland grasses had been planted over the years to help keep down the cheatgrass that always wanted to take over any cleared area. Even with the constant fight to eradicate it, there were patches of cheatgrass scattered here and there. Patches of sagebrush had also re-emerged in places between the pinon and juniper trees that dotted the pasture. The entire pasture was surrounded by a five-foot-high, four rail fence that had been very carefully maintained for a full century. It was impossible not to notice the varying ages of the lodgepole and spruce rails that the fence was made of. Some of the rails and a few of the cedar posts had obviously been recently replaced, and then there were others that appeared to be as old as the BR itself.

It wasn't hard to talk Anna into taking him across the river. He had been a little bit embarrassed about having to ride behind a girl, but the thrill of sitting directly behind Anna and being able to put his arms around her middle to hold on as they crossed the river easily outweighed any embarrassment he might have felt. Once again, they had faced the dilemma of how they were going to get away from Ralph and Cody, but that dilemma had been solved by Clyde asking the boys to help him repair some breaks in the barbed wire fence around the big meadow to the north.

At the entrance to the south pasture, somewhat reluctantly, James slid off of Pintada. He planned on opening the gate to let Anna ride through. He was surprised when she also dismounted.

"I can open the gate for you", he said.

"No need," Anna replied. "We can just climb over. We have to leave Pintada here."

"Why?" James asked. He had thought they would just ride up to the horses in the south pasture to get a good close look at all of them.

Anna scowled a little. She was hesitant and a little embarrassed as to how she should answer. "Grullo is in there, and Pintada's in heat." She blushed as she said it, and wondered at James' lack of knowledge of the natural world in general, and the mating habits of horses, in particular. *Such a city boy*, she thought.

She tied her horse to one of the fence rails next to the gate that led into the pasture. Not bothering to open the gate, they both just climbed over. They couldn't see any of the horses from here, they must have been in one of the bottoms behind the hill that was immediately in front of them. They made the short climb to the top of the hill and looked down to the east end of the pasture. Spider Creek swung to the south at that corner of the pasture, and a portion of the fence had been built out into the creek creating a natural watering hole for the horses. The herd was spread out near the river contentedly eating the grass that was plentiful in the bottom. There were eight horses that were visible from their vantage point. Most of the horses were bays or sorrels. There was one buckskin colored horse and one pure black one. That had to be the horse Chuck had warned James about. There was also one big silvery gray grazing somewhat apart from the rest of the herd, as though he was a sentinel.

That has to be Grullo, James thought. "Is that all of them," he asked.

"I'm not sure, but I think so. Is your grandpa really going to give you one of those horses?" she asked, at least a hint of skepticism in her voice.

"Whichever one I want." It was almost a brag. "All I have to do is pick one out and catch it. Grandpa did say I should probably stay away from the black one, though."

Anna furrowed her eyebrows. "Why did he want you to stay away from Midnight," she asked. "He's my favorite."

"I don't know. Maybe he doesn't trust him." Even as he said it, he began having doubts. Maybe the black one, Midnight, is Grandpa's favorite, too. Maybe he wants to keep him for himself. That didn't make sense either. Chuck seemed perfectly happy with the big bay horse called Red that he always rode.

Most of the horses were about a hundred yards away, down the hill below where James and Anna sat watching them. Partially concealed by a juniper tree, and downwind from the herd, none of the horses had shown any sign of noticing them yet. The big silver-gray called Grullo was closest to them and seemed totally outstanding to James.

"Maybe I'll catch Grullo," he said quietly.

Once again, Anna was incredulous; amazed at James' innocence and ignorance. "You can't choose Grullo! He's the stallion."

She must have said it louder than she intended. Grullo lifted his head and turned toward them, his full attention, eyes, ears, and nose focused on the top of the hill where they sat. Both Anna and James froze instinctively. Grullo studied the two for a few seconds before his attention was pulled away from the hill by a scent in the air coming from the herd below him. Sticking his nose in the air and turning his head toward the rest of the horses, he took off at a trot, headed directly for the buckskin mare standing a little apart from the rest of the herd. As Grullo approached the mare, his penis started extending below his abdomen, getting longer and longer. The mare, with an air of indifference, seemed to be ignoring his approach. Right up to the point where Grullo stuck his nose up under her tail, that is. She jumped a little then, turning her rear away from Grullo. He, in turn, stuck his nose straight up into the air with his teeth bared in what appeared to be a huge smile. As he did so, his penis, which had been dangling mostly straight down rose toward his belly in anticipation. He moved toward the rear of the mare. She started to turn away again with a little kick half-heartedly aimed his way. Not taking no for an answer, Grullo nipped the base of her neck and moved to mount her. Now the mare acquiesced, as James and Anna watched spellbound.

James had never personally witnessed animals breeding before, and though Anna had seen it many times, she hadn't intimately watched with a boy by her side, and she hadn't been well on her way to womanhood. Though neither yet knew what eroticism was, it was a weirdly erotic experience for both of them. Both were flushed and just sat there in silence, afraid to do or say anything.

Anna, fully aware of the strange feelings stirring in her lower belly, was the first to speak. "Have you ever thought about us doing that?" she asked.

James had thought about it alright, but he had no idea if he could actually do it. He didn't know what to say. Finally, he decided it best to just change the subject to something he was more equipped to deal with. "Why do you think Grandpa told me to stay away from Midnight?" he asked.

Anna, both relieved and a little disappointed at the change of subject, thought about it and had the answer. "He thought telling you to stay away from Midnight would make you want to own him."

James realized immediately that she was right. "Okay, that settles it, I'm going to catch Midnight." He thought about for a bit, and then said, "How can I do that?"

"Come on, I'll help you. We need to get some oats," Anna said, as she stood up. She took James hand as they walked back down the hill toward Pintada.

Something happened on that hill that neither James nor Anna could ever explain. An innocence between them had been lost forever.

Chapter 3

The one conference room at the Kremmling Hotel was already getting crowded when Chuck arrived. Tables had been arranged in a semi-circle with a small stage and dais in the front of the room. Chuck spotted John Crowley sitting at a table near the center of the room with an empty chair next to him.

"Hey John, is this spot taken?" Chuck asked, tapping John on the shoulder.

"Hi, neighbor. No, Martha didn't want to attend. She didn't know if she could stand to sit through a sales presentation, especially one sponsored by the USDA. Sit down. Do you happen to know any more about this than I do?"

"Guess not. I must've got the same notice as everyone else. Looks like every cattle rancher in the area's here. Have to wonder what the Department of Ag is up to; basically, ordering us to a meeting with something called Pro Foods. Probably can't be a good thing; not with the feds involved."

"Kind of what I've been thinking," John said, fidgeting with his water glass. "Do you know anything about Pro Foods?"

"Not really. Other than they apparently want to buy all the cattle we can produce."

A man stepped forward from the other side of the room and strode to a position behind the dais. He was a fairly short man, but the boots he was wearing made him a little taller. The boots, bolo tie, and the western jacket seemed out of place on the man; and the Stetson hat was about as fitting to this man's head as the deer antlers on a jackalope.

"Good morning," his voice boomed out of the speakers, as he removed the Stetson and placed it on the dais. The light reflected off the top of his bald head when he bent down to adjust the volume on the PA system. "For those of you that I have yet to meet, my name is Bud Johnson, and, as you probably already know, I represent Pro Foods."

With the small talk around the room ended, and everyone's attention on Bud Johnson, he went on; "you're probably wondering what is Pro Foods? And what the hell does the USDA have to do with it?" With that, he touched another button on the dais and the screen above and behind him sprang to life. Listed down the left side of the screen were the names of most of the major food producers in the U.S.; General Mills, Tyson Foods, Kellogg's, Dole, etc. On the right side there were four letters in bold type; USDA. Each of the food company names had a line running from it to a point centered on the USDA.

"Pro Foods is a private-public partnership whose mission is to alleviate hunger in this country." Bud Johnson went on to explain to those gathered that the cuts to social security and other social programs that were forced on the Federal Government by the economic collapse known as the *Catastrophe*, had left many Americans with "food insecurities"; and how the USDA had partnered with all of "these fine companies" to make sure that all Americans at least had food to eat.

There was, of course, not a single person in the room that was unaware of the starvation going on across the country. Many of the ranchers in the room had insecurities themselves. Unlike Chuck, most of the ranchers here, as elsewhere in the country, had been deeply in debt when the Catastrophe hit; and the austerity measures imposed by the good ole Federal Government had left a lot of them in dire straits financially. Most of everything they produced went to prop up the banks and the economic elite that controlled their debt. If not for their ability to grow a lot of their own food, they would have been as bad off as so many of the people living in squalor in the cities.

Chuck Pierson was far better off than most. Unlike most of the other ranchers in the room, Chuck not only owned all of the land that the BR sat on, he owned the mineral rights for the gas and oil that lay beneath the land. Most of the mineral rights in this part of Colorado had been sold for lump-sum payments back in the 1950s and '60s. Back then, the speculators were offering thousands of dollars for mineral deeds and the ranchers were going broke. It seemed stupid not to take the cash; especially before fracking when it seemed that the oil and gas below their land would just stay below their land forever. Charles Pierson senior, Charlie to everyone who knew him, Chuck's father, hadn't seen it that way. He'd refused to sell any part of his mineral rights and he'd managed to hold onto the BR through decades of hard times. When the fracking boom took off in the 1990s, the Blue River Ranch was one of the first places drilled. Charles senior had lived long enough to see the royalties start coming in, and those royalties had grown to become Chuck's main source of income. The BR was indeed a cattle ranch, and Chuck loved ranching, but up until recent times, the BR had been as much about oil and gas as it was about cattle. The income from oil and gas had just about dried up, though. Especially the crude oil income, which was by far the most lucrative. It wasn't that the wells had gone dry, there was still plenty of oil down there; it was the demand for oil that was drying up. The world was shifting away from oil just like the world had shifted away from coal. Chuck had mixed feelings about the shift from fossil fuels to green energy. Climate change could no longer be denied, not with all the weather-related disasters increasing at an exponential pace, but keeping the BR financially viable by raising cattle was definitely not easy.

"We, at the USDA, working with the private sector, have developed Allpro," Bud Johnson continued his spiel, as a new image flashed on the screen above him. The image on the screen appeared to be some kind of meatloaf on a platter with basic nutrition information spelled out below the picture. From the nutrition info, it appeared that three servings of this Allpro would provide nearly a hundred percent of a person's daily nutrition needs. "Since the government can no longer afford to provide monetary food assistance to those in need, we will provide the food instead. Instead of monetary assistance to buy whatever food people choose to eat, those in need will receive vouchers to purchase Allpro. Once the program is fully implemented, no one in this country will ever need to go hungry again."

"Doesn't appear to have missed too many meals, himself, does he," John half-whispered to Chuck.

"And this is where you come in," Bud continued, gesturing to the entire room. "Allpro is a complete food product that contains all of the carbohydrates, fats, and proteins that a person needs to survive; along with vitamins and minerals. It is made from a combination of fruits, vegetables, and meats. It will be produced by the fine companies listed earlier in plants scattered around the country. Here's the interesting thing; nearly any kind of meat can be used. We plan to use a combination of chicken, pork, turkey, and beef; but there's one problem. Beef is simply too expensive. Protein from plants, pork, and especially poultry, is much more economical."

That brought a grumbling murmur to the room. It had been years since anyone had made any money off of their cattle. Even before the Catastrophe, the independent ranchers weren't making money by selling beef. The only ones making any money off of cattle were the very companies who were now, it seemed to many in the room, taking over the USDA.

"Wait a minute," a loud voice spoke up from somewhere behind Chuck and John. "I thought you said you wanted to buy our cattle."

Chuck turned to see that the speaker was Neil Smith. Neil owned a small spread up in the northwest corner of Grand County. *He probably doesn't have more than a hundred head to sell*, Chuck thought. And then the thought struck him that he had reduced the size of his own herd to the point where he wouldn't be able to sell a whole lot more than that, either. This definitely wasn't the good old days when the BR ran a herd that numbered in the thousands. In the years since the Catastrophe, the number of people who could afford to eat beef had gone steadily down, and those who could still afford a good steak had mostly stopped eating beef altogether to help fight climate change. As the demand for beef declined, so did the price that ranchers were paid at market. Chuck had reduced the size of the herd on the BR to around two hundred head, less than ten percent of what had been the norm back in the day. If not for the fact that he loved ranching, and the responsibility he felt to provide a place for Clyde Duran and his family to live and work, he might have sold his entire herd. The royalties on gas and oil were still enough to support one man.

"Pro Foods does want to buy your cattle," Bud answered. "Right now, we need all the cattle we can get, but I need to warn you that isn't going to be the case forever. The long-range plan is to phase out cattle altogether. They're too expensive. Short term, we're phasing out feedlots. They're too hard on the environment and besides, if beef is only a source of protein, it isn't going to matter if it's tender or not. We do want to buy your cattle, that's a fact. But the government, I mean Pro Foods, can't pay market price."

At that, the murmur in the room turned into a roar. Some of the ranchers were standing and yelling at Bud Johnson. Others were still seated, but everyone was angry. "What do you mean market price," someone shouted. "What market?" Another voice yelled out, "First you cut our subsidies and now you want to steal our cattle!" That comment referenced the fact that the latest farm bill had reduced the subsidies that the federal government provided to the agricultural community. Those government subsidies were the only thing that kept many of these ranchers in business.

Bud Johnson stood stoically behind the dais, allowing the questions and verbal abuse to wash over him and slowly subside. Chuck realized it was the reaction that Bud had expected. This obviously wasn't the first group he'd been sent to coerce into accepting Pro Food's plan.

As the roar from the crowd slowly died down, Bud Johnson resumed speaking. "Here's the deal, and this is the true bottom line; the SNAP program is going away. It is not going to be simply reduced further, it is going to be eliminated entirely. Now, I know that demand for your beef cattle has diminished over the past few years, and prices have gone down. But you have to realize that what demand there is, has been propped up by the government giving people the means to buy beef if they so desire. The SNAP program will end in about three months. It will be replaced by a new program, Allpro For All, AFA for short, that will allow the federal government to continue providing nutrition to those Americans in need."

The ranchers had grown quiet as Bud was speaking. Most were looking at him now with a mixture of disgust and dejection; first-hand witnesses to the ongoing breakdown of the U.S. Federal Government.

"Unlike food stamp programs of the past, AFA vouchers can only be used to purchase Allpro, nothing else. Production and distribution facilities for Allpro are ramping up as I speak so there will be plenty available as soon as the program takes effect. We need your beef production to start shipping to the processing plants as soon as possible and we'll be paying you seventy-five percent of current market prices for every pound you ship."

Anger, once again, ran through the crowd. "Are you crazy, you son of a bitch," it was Neil Smith again. "I wouldn't sell to you if you were the last buyer on earth."

"Who the hell do you think you are?" Chuck didn't recognize that voice, but the general din in the room was drowning it out, anyway.

Once again, Bud Johnson simply stood his place waiting for the eruption to end. As the room slowly quieted down, a sad look came over him. "It isn't me," he said solemnly into the microphone. "You have to understand that it isn't me. I understand your anger. I'm angry, too. I can't stand the fact that a few fat cats in Washington have bankrupted our country and driven common people to the point of starvation. But I believe this is the only way to prevent those common people from actually starving. There are no other options. And, as much as I have no other options, neither do you. The USDA is prepared to end all agricultural subsidies to any farmer or rancher who refuses to join the program."

Chuck sat silently in his seat, his emotions perfectly masked. He felt anger, along with everyone else in the room; but he had a deeper sense of sadness than he did of anger. He realized the sadness came from a lifetime of watching the decline of America. It wasn't just the *fat cats* in Washington, as Bud Johnson had put it. It was the system that had put them there. It was the system that produced the ever-widening gap between the haves and the have nots. For a time, it had seemed like the Catastrophe had somewhat leveled the playing field, but Chuck knew that was not really the case. The haves still had, and now, five years after the Catastrophe, they were still rigging the system. He actually felt sorry for Bud Johnson standing there taking the verbal abuse. Bud actually believed that he was on a mission to save people from starving. Chuck wondered if Bud had even considered what was in it for the food companies that had gone along with this plan. *Gone along with it, hell,* he thought; *they're the ones that put the whole thing together.* He stood up and took a look around at the rest of the ranchers who were mostly also standing and yelling; demanding more from Bud Johnson and the Federal Government than they were ever going to get. Without saying a word, Chuck Pierson turned and walked slowly, deliberately out the door. He suddenly wanted nothing more than to be home, alone, on the Blue River Ranch.

After luring Midnight with a bucket of oats and getting him in a halter, James and Anna had led him back to the log barn and put him in one of the stalls. They had then climbed to the loft, broken one of the bales of hay and dropped about half of it through the hole in the floor into the stall's manger.

"Thanks, Anna." James had said, as he had put his hands on her shoulders and kissed her for the second time. Their kiss this time was somehow not as magical as their first, but definitely more natural. Their heads seemed to both know which way to turn and their lips lingered together longer. Then they heard the distinct sound of Chuck's big diesel pickup coming up the lane.

Chuck had parked his truck in the metal shop where he always did and headed straight to the house. James ran after him but didn't catch up until Chuck was already in the house sitting at his big desk.

"You caught Midnight!" Chuck exclaimed, with mock surprise. "All by yourself?"

"Anna helped me." James was reluctant to tell his Grandpa that Anna had actually done most of the catching. "But now that I've caught him, can Midnight really be mine?"

"Well…I guess a deal's a deal. Can you ride him?"

"I haven't ridden him yet, but I'm sure I can. He seems as gentle as Pintada. Can we go for a ride now?" James asked, even though he could see that Chuck seemed to be concentrating on the screen in front of him.

For a moment it seemed that Chuck hadn't even heard the question, but then he turned and smiled at his only grandson. The smile was warm, but there was a kind of sadness in his eyes.

"I can't go for a ride right now James, it's getting late and I have some work that I have to do in here."

"Maybe me and Anna can go for a ride. It won't be dinner time for a while."

"I really think you'd better wait to throw a saddle on Midnight until I can help. Tell you what, if you can find something else to do this evening, I promise we can go for a good long ride first thing tomorrow morning."

James disappointment was evident, but he could see that Chuck had already made up his mind. "Okay," he said, "but remember, you promised to go in the morning. Come on Anna, let's go take care of our horses," he said as he turned and saw Anna standing behind him.

"Hey, if you two see Clyde out there, tell him I need to see him," Chuck called after them, as they headed out the door. Then, muttering "never mind" to himself, he grabbed his comphone and told it to call Clyde.

Clyde found Chuck still sitting at his desk, still studying the screen in front of him. "Grab a chair," was the only thing Chuck said to Clyde, as he stared at the screen. He had been researching everything he could find about Pro Foods, and what he found was troubling, to say the least. It brought a combination of feelings of anger and helplessness. He felt helpless to change what he saw as the downward spiral of the country that he loved, and the more helpless he felt, the angrier he became. At some point in his life, the United States had been stricken with a disease, like a cancer. He couldn't say when the cancer had started growing, and he couldn't say specifically what the cancer was. Was it greed for money? Or, for power? Was it a lack of morals or religion? Maybe too much religion or, more precisely, greed for religious power. Whatever the cancer was that had started growing long ago, it wasn't Pro Foods; but Pro Foods was definitely proof that the cancer had metastasized. The Catastrophe had surely been evidence of the cancer's spread throughout the economy. Pro Foods was proof positive that the cancer had now spread throughout the Federal Government as well.

Since the Catastrophe, every social program under the sun had been slashed or privatized, or both. The privatization of Social Security and subsequent slashing of benefits had been especially hard on Chuck's generation. It had meant starvation and homelessness for way too many elderly Americans. And what had really galled Chuck about it more than anything else, was the knowledge that it had helped enrich his son in law, Robert James Mendez – investment banking guru. And now, Chuck had found, among all of the other information about Pro Foods a list of the board of directors. One name stood out on that list and Chuck just kept staring at it, his mind in turmoil. One name; Robert James Mendez.

"What's up, meeting in town didn't go well?" Clyde's question brought Chuck's attention back to the present.

"No, the meeting didn't go well at all. Stealing cash through taxes wasn't enough. Now, they want our cattle, too."

Clyde looked at the screen that Chuck had been staring at. The heading at the top said, Pro-Foods Corporate Structure. There was a sub-heading below that, Corporate Ownership. Instead of listing the owners, however, there was a statement to the effect that Pro Foods was a private corporation that was jointly owned by the USDA and private interests. Since it was a private, not public, corporation, those private interests were left undisclosed. There was, however, a listing of the Board of Directors, noting how these prominent benefactors were giving their time and efforts to further the cause of ending hunger in America once and for all. Clyde, of course, noticed the inclusion of James' father on that list.

A quick cynical smile played across Clyde's face. "So, not quite as altruistic as they're made out to be, eh?"

"Altruistic my ass!" That scum-bag son-in-law of mine doesn't do anything unless there's money it for him. "Ending hunger - Bullshit!"

Good thing James isn't here, Clyde thought. It was, of course, no secret that Chuck Pierson had no use for Noni's husband Robert. He wondered again, as he had many times over the past fifteen years, why Noni had married Robert Mendez. His thoughts started to turn toward fond memories of his youth, growing up with Noni here on the ranch. Those thoughts were interrupted by Chuck.

"We're going to lose our agricultural fuel subsidies, Clyde. Worse than that, I'm afraid we're going to lose the market for our cattle." Chuck went on to explain the details of the meeting in town. How Pro Foods was going to monopolize food production and how they were trying to set themselves up as the only market for beef, pork, turkey and chickens. How they were going to supply a single food item called Allpro.

"Nicely named," Clyde said. "Kind of like that old dog food, Alpo. Probably tastes about the same, too."

Chuck had to smile at that. "Yeah, I'm sure it isn't going to taste anything like a good old rib-eye, is it?"

Clyde thought about it for a second or two and, as usual, saw things differently than Chuck, or most people for that matter. "That's why we won't lose our market," he said. "You think Robert Mendez is going to eat dog food? Sure, there're millions of people who won't have a choice, but there are more than a few rich people that won't be giving up beef steaks anytime soon."

He's right, Chuck thought; as long as there's a one percent or a one-tenth of one percent, there will be a market. Even if the feds outlaw it, there'll be a black market. The rich are going to get what they want one way or another. And, we can get by without the fuel subsidies. We'll just have to cut our fuel use even more than we already have.

The two men discussed the situation some more and decided that they would have to cut the size of the herd down to about a hundred head. That would allow them to lay off the two hands that were up in the high country with the cattle. Chuck and the Duran family could manage the rest of the herd by themselves. Anna, Ralph, and Cody were all old enough to help, and maybe they could get James to help out, at least in the summer. *That'd be a good slap in Robert Mendez' face,* Chuck thought.

"Thinking about it that way," Clyde said, "maybe after Pro Foods locks down the regular markets, beef on the outside of those markets might be worth a whole lot more."

That's when it dawned on Chuck that Clyde was right about steak being worth a whole lot more once the market was locked up, but it wouldn't be ranchers raking in the profit. It would be the Pro Foods investors. They had rigged the system, rigged the government to monopolize the foods produced by independent farmers and ranchers so they could rake in even more money than they already did. There would still be steak and chicken and anything else available to those who could afford it. And there would be Allpro available for those who couldn't. Pro Foods would be the only market that ranchers could sell their beef cattle to, and they would set the price however low they liked, but you could bet your bottom dollar that all of that beef wasn't going into Allpro. There would be a hidden branch or subsidiary, or maybe more than one, that would get the best cuts of beef and the best parts of the chickens and hogs. Those would be sold at a huge profit, and they wouldn't be labeled *Pro Foods.* No, Allpro, that wonder food for the masses, that salvation for the starving - Allpro wouldn't contain the steaks and chops and chicken breasts. Allpro would get the beaks and feet, the hooves and hides, and whatever other parts they could turn into protein meal.

"You're right, Clyde. They will lock down the markets, but they're not going to allow any other market to compete with 'em, either. There'll still be steaks available for Robert Mendez and friends, but they'll be the ones selling those, too. They just won't say Pro Foods on the label."

Clyde could see that Chuck was absolutely right. Pro Foods wasn't a power play to monopolize a part of the food market. Pro Foods was a power play to monopolize all of the food market. "Guess we don't have any choice but to sign up," he said. "At least if we sign up, we'll get to keep our fuel subsidies."

There is that, Chuck thought. As much as he hated being any part of it, they only had two choices. Sign on to the Pro Foods market, or stop raising cattle altogether. *If we stop altogether,* he thought, *they'll probably just confiscate the ranch. If they can steal our cattle, they can just as easily steal our land. All they'd have to do is say it was for the "greater good". Once again, he had a thought that he'd had many times over the course of his life – we need a revolution. That's what this country really needs; a revolution. Hell, it's not just this country, the whole goddamned world needs a revolution.*

Chuck slid a finger across the screen in front of them and a Pro Foods contract appeared on the screen. "I guess that's settled then. As much as I hate to, I'll sign this damn contract. Guess it's better than shutting down or losing the ranch."

It was still early in the morning; James was already in the log barn putting the saddle and bridle on Midnight, something he had done many times over the past several weeks. He had come to think of the horse as a friend more than a possession. He and Anna had ridden nearly every day since the capture of Midnight. *Where is she*, he thought; this is our last day. Tomorrow, Grandpa Chuck would take him to Kremmling and put him on the train, they only had one more day to spend together.

The past few weeks had been quite an emotional roller coaster for James. From the highs of time spent with Anna, to the lows of overheard arguments between his dad and his grandfather. He wasn't very anxious to get home to Castle Pines. He was afraid his father would never let him come back to the ranch. But at the same time, he didn't understand why his grandfather seemed to dislike his father so much. To James, his father was very successful and had always provided James and his mother with everything they could ask for; and yet, this very success was what Chuck seemed to dislike. It was something that was totally beyond his understanding. Grandpa Chuck certainly wasn't poor or deprived, and yet he seemed to have a general dislike for the truly wealthy, just as that salesman on the train, Bud Johnson, had seemed to disdain the wealthy.

James remembered how, when he was younger, he and his Mom had spent a lot of time here at the BR. There had been so many visits that he couldn't remember them all, but his father rarely accompanied them. From summer vacations to holidays, those were mostly all happy memories for James. As he thought about it, James realized that the last time his father had driven them out to Kremmling was when his grandmother died. That was three years ago. Grandma Nancy had died of some kind of cancer at a young age. His mind didn't exactly frame it that way, but James couldn't help but wonder now whether Grandpa Chuck somehow blamed his Grandma's death on the wealthy. His Mom didn't, of that he was sure. This was the first year that she hadn't driven him out to the ranch for his summer vacation, let alone, not even driving out to pick him up. He was sure that she wanted to see Grandpa, and that she loved spending time here at her childhood home, and yet, Grandpa would be putting him on the train tomorrow. He wondered what it meant that his Mom wouldn't be driving out to pick him up.

"Hi, James." The sound of Anna's voice startled him as he was tightening the cinch. He hadn't even heard her come into the barn.

"Morning Anna." His face brightened into a big smile as he spoke. "Where should we go today?"

Anna just said, "I don't know," as she grabbed the bridle and headed to Pintada's stall. James looked after her, the smile fading from his eyes as he realized she was not in a very good mood at all. Come to think of it, he wasn't really in a very good mood himself. *Guess it's just that this is my last day,* he thought.

As it turned out, they mostly just rode about somewhat aimlessly. They rode up to the ranch cemetery, which sat on a hill just to the west of the old homestead. It was a pretty morning view from there, with the sun just a little way up the sky and the headquarters of the BR spread out below them. They lingered there for a little, looking at the headstones marking the graves of both of their ancestors. Each having grandparents and great grandparents buried in the same cemetery seemed to be another link joining them together.

From the cemetery, they rode on up to the big mesa to the west. Riding side by side up the steep two track road that wound its way through the scrub oak, they emerged onto the large gently sloping expanse of cleared pasture. A good part of the big mesa was irrigated hay meadow. The part that wasn't irrigated was mostly sagebrush, with a few pinon and juniper trees scattered here and there.

The knee-high grasses in the irrigated meadow waved in the breeze, like gently lapping waves on a large lake. As they emerged from the scrub oak, which grew all around the mesa's flanks, they startled three buck deer that had been eating the bounty at the edge of the meadow. If you didn't know it already, you could tell the season of the year by simply seeing the bucks grazing peacefully together in the grass hay that was ready for harvest. Having the bucks together, not yet in rut, said that it wasn't yet fall; and seeing that the hay was ready to mow said that summer was almost over. *Just like my vacation is almost over*, James thought.

From the big mesa, they forded Spider Creek, which was a really small stream this late in the summer. Very little snow had fallen in the mountains during the previous winter; the ongoing drought in this part of the country was extreme, to say the least. Even though the BR had the most senior water rights of any ranch around, they hadn't been able to irrigate as much as Grandpa Chuck would have liked.

After crossing the creek, James and Anna followed a series of game and cattle trails winding their way back down through the scrub oak to the southeast. Emerging from a particularly thick stand of brush, they found themselves at the gate to the south pasture where they had caught Midnight just a few weeks ago. Just a few weeks that seemed like forever, on the one hand, and like the blink of an eye on the other. Without saying a word, Anna swung down out of the saddle, and with practiced ease, held the reins of Pintada while opening the gate.

"Isn't Grullo still in there?" James asked as Anna led Pintada through the gate.

"Yes," Anna answered. "But Pintada isn't in heat now."

She wondered if James would ever be observant enough, when it came to a mare, to know when one was in heat. *Probably not,* she thought. *He didn't grow up around horses like I did.*

James rode through the gate, and Anna closed it behind them. She didn't get back on Pintada, though; just started walking, leading the paint. James decided that maybe he should dismount as well, wondering about the strange mood that seemed to have come over Anna. *Actually, Anna had been acting strangely all day*, he thought. Then he thought about his own feelings, this final day before he had to go home to Castle Pines. It wasn't that he didn't want to go home, he just wished that Anna could somehow go with him. It was a totally irrational thought, but he knew he liked being with Anna more than any of his friends back home. Knowing that he now missed his Dad, and especially, his Mom didn't diminish the fact that he knew he would miss Anna a lot.

They led their horses in silence, walking side by side, and found themselves on top of the hill where they had sat just a few weeks before; young voyeurs watching horses in the intimate act of breeding.

Anna didn't say anything, she just took the lunch she had brought from her saddlebag and removed the bridle from Pintada so she could also eat without the bit in her mouth. James followed suit, also in silence. They let the horses go about the business of grazing freely, it wasn't like they could get too far away, and sat together in very nearly the same spot they had sat before.

This time none of the other horses were visible from where they sat. They must have been behind the hill to the south. The two of them sat side by side on the grass, eating their lunch in awkward silence. Anna finally broke the silence.

"I don't want you to go." It was a simple statement, spoken in her soft matter of fact way. "I'm afraid you won't come back."

James swallowed the apple he'd been chewing. "I'll be back, I always get to come back." He wished he was as sure as he sounded. He put his arm around Anna. She leaned against him. They sat in silence, watching a bald eagle as it rode the thermals and slowly floated down to land on one of the large cottonwood trees that grew along the river. For some reason, the eagle gave James a sense of unease, a foreboding feeling that he couldn't quite put his finger on. Truth be known, he too, was afraid he wouldn't be coming back.

PART TWO

A Chinese man dressed in modern business attire sits behind a desk in a large starkly furnished office in Zhongnanhai in Beijing. There is a knock on the door, and then, before the man even answers the knock, another man dressed in a Chinese military uniform steps briskly through the door. He stops, standing at attention in front of the desk. He speaks just a few words in Mandarin, salutes, pivots and walks back out the door, closing it quietly behind him.

The man sitting at the desk reaches down and plucks an antique telephone receiver off of its cradle. Holding the antique to his ear with one hand, he pushes a series of numbers on the phone's keypad with the other. After a few moments of silence, someone obviously picks up on the other end of the antiquated landline. The Chinese man speaks one sentence into the phone. Incongruously, it is spoken in perfect Farsi. Just one short sentence; "It is done." Without saying another word, the man slowly lowers the phone back into its cradle.

Chapter 4

Snow was falling outside the window of his room on the fourth floor of the dorm. It was early January, James was a high school sophomore at Colorado One on the north side of Boulder. This was his second year at the new Colorado boarding school which specialized in a highly tailored STEM curriculum. "Unequalled Excellence In Education" was the school's motto. The unequal part was certainly accurate. The school only admitted the most economically elite students. It was said, in a new take on an old saying, that if you had to ask what the cost of tuition was, you couldn't afford it. Classes would resume tomorrow, James was just settling in after being dropped off by Don. Robert hadn't been able to accompany James to Boulder because of a "crucial" meeting he had to attend at his office, and his mother had come down with the flu or something over the holidays.

Just as well, he thought. Sometimes it seemed like he enjoyed Don's company more than the company of his parents, anyway. Don was a friendly companion, as much as he was a bodyguard. Next month James would be fifteen, then he could get an Autonomous Vehicle operator's license and "drive" himself wherever he wanted to go. Where he'd wanted to go for Christmas was out to the Blue River Ranch. Once again, that had not been allowed. James had not been allowed to go visit his Grandpa for over two years now. Grandpa Chuck and the Blue River Ranch were hardly ever even mentioned in the presence of his father. James knew that his mother still kept in touch with Grandpa Chuck, but that part of her life was a taboo subject around Robert Mendez. Likewise, James always kept in touch with Anna, but the less his mom and dad knew about it, the better.

Feeling the comphone in his pocket vibrate, James pulled it out and folded it open. Anna was on screen, looking as great as always. James had to wonder if she made herself up before calling, or just looked that good all the time. He touched the screen to allow his image to be seen and smiled brightly into the camera.

"Hi Anna, I was just thinking about you." Truth be known, James thought about Anna most of the time.

"Hi James, are you back at school yet?" She knew he was; otherwise, he would've answered with a text instead of voice video.

By way of answer, James, who was standing with his back to the window, raised the com up above his head letting Anna see the view. "How are you?" he asked, bringing the com back down to face level. "Did you have a good Christmas?"

"I didn't get what I wanted for Christmas," she pouted. "I thought you were going to come see me."

The smile in her eyes belied her pouting lips and James had to laugh. "You know I wanted to," he teased.

Anna's pout turned into a radiant smile. "When is your Dad going to let you come back? I might get another boyfriend if you make me wait too long."

"Maybe this summer; I'll be fifteen. Maybe I'll just come out there whether my Dad wants me to or not." James tried to sound more confident than he was.

Anna started to reply and then vanished. The screen simply went blank. James looked at the status bar; no signal. *That's odd*, he thought. "Hey Assie, what's wrong with my com?" He'd considered naming his digital assistant simply Ass but had decided to lengthen it to Assie after his Mom protested him walking around the house saying *Hey Ass* all the time. There was no reply from his digital assistant. He walked over to the desk and looked down at the DA speaker. The green power light was glowing steady, meaning it definitely had power. What the heck is going on, he thought, as he reached down and pushed the power button. When in doubt, reboot. It was something he'd learned at a very early age. The power light flashed red, then yellow, and finally achieved a steady green glow, as the DA speaker powered up. The green light came on, but there was no familiar greeting from Assie, only silence.

Knowing that the artificial intelligence used by Assie wasn't in the little round speaker on the desk, but rather in massive servers located who knew where, James didn't bother asking Assie to turn on the comscreen on the wall above his desk. Instead, he reached up and manually pushed the comscreen's power button. Like the DA, the comscreen powered up just fine, but instead of his usual home screen, there were just two words in bold red caps in the middle of the screen; NO CONNECTION.

James stared at the screen for a few moments. It seemed almost incomprehensible. *How could there be no connection?* The internet linked everything. It had been totally secure since the government made it that way in the wake of foreign interference in the elections of 2016 and 2018, and especially after all of the social media problems of 2020. He turned away from the screen and looked out his window again. The view from his fourth-floor window was to the east. Across the grounds of Colorado One, he could see the tall security fence that ran completely around the school's grounds. Just on the other side of the fence, Highway 36 ran its north-south route between Boulder and Lyons. Highway 36, which usually had quite a bit of traffic moving in both directions now looked more like a parking lot than a highway. There were a few vehicles still moving, mostly along the shoulders and even down in the borrow ditches, but the main traffic lanes were entirely jammed by cars and trucks that were all stopped haphazardly; looking for all the world like everyone had simultaneously shut down their vehicles in the middle of the highway.

As he looked at the chaos on Highway 36, James realized that the only vehicles that were still moving were older cars and trucks that were actually driven by a human driver and not dependent on artificial intelligence and GPS guidance. He could see more and more of the older vehicles trying to work their way out of the stalled traffic and onto the shoulders and down into the borrow ditches, but none of the newer autonomous vehicles were moving at all.

It was getting to be late afternoon, and most of the Colorado One students were settling into their dorms for the new trimester, just as James was doing. There were a few who were just arriving, and a few more were in some of the vehicles that were stalled all over the highway. As James headed to the stairs, he wasn't about to try the elevators, he passed by a window at the end of the hallway with a view of the main entry gates to the school. The gates were made of wrought iron and were opened and closed by the security guards that manned the four guard stations; two guard stations on each side of the ten-foot security fence that surrounded the school. Both the entrance and exit gates were standing open. There was a Mercedes EV blocking the entrance gate and one of the new Jaguars blocking the exit. All eight members of the security guard regiment were milling about the two stalled vehicles with their assault rifles slung over their shoulders. It was obviously not an attack on the school, and there was nothing threatening in sight; other than the eight armed guards at the security gates, that is.

James wasn't the only student who had ventured down to the lobby common area to try to find out what was going on. The dorm building was actually like two separate four-story apartment buildings with a common area between them on the ground floor that housed the lobby, cafeteria, and a large student lounge. The north wing housed the boy's dorms and the south wing housed the girl's. The lobby, cafeteria, and student lounge were shared in the large single-story common area. Boys were not allowed in the girl's wing, and girls were not allowed in the boy's, which made life a little bit tricky for the LGBT students. They were generally placed according to their self-identified gender. James thought they probably should have built a third wing so they could have male, female, and other or undecided.

As James stepped out of the stairwell into the lobby, there were a lot more people than the few dating couples who were usually milling around.

There were almost as many students in the common area lounge as there were in the cafeteria on pizza days. Most, if not all, were wearing questioning expressions and talking among themselves. It was obvious that they had no more idea of what was going on than James did. As he looked around, he saw a girl that he hadn't seen before standing by herself off to the side of the main entrance doors. She was standing a little behind the schefflera plant in its large pot, which partially shielded her from his view and provided her some separation from the rest of the students. She was holding something to her ear with one hand. James couldn't tell what it was. He worked his way through the gathering crowd to get closer. As he approached her, he could see that whatever it was she was holding to her ear looked like nothing more than a small black plastic box.

"Hi," James said as he approached the girl. As she looked up at him, he was somewhat taken aback at the extremely concerned look on her face. He also couldn't help but notice in that first instant of eye contact how attractive she was. Her hair was that strawberry blonde color that isn't quite blonde and not quite red. She had a very fair, almost pale, complexion, and her eyes were the clearest blue.

"Oh, hello," she said, never lowering the plastic box from her ear. A smile never even flashed across her face, the ultra-concerned look seeming as permanent as the black plastic box that was stuck to her ear.

"I'm James," he said, trying to get more of a conversation started than just *hello*. "What are you listening to?"

The girl slowly lowered her hand holding what James could now tell was some kind of antique radio thing. As she pulled it away from her ear, he could hear a voice coming out of it. He couldn't make out all of the words, which was obviously why the girl had been holding it up to her ear. He thought he made out the words, *emergency alert*, but he couldn't be sure.

"It's the emergency alert system." The way she said it, she might as well have added, *you idiot*, but she didn't. She also didn't smile, and James was about to just walk away when she added, "I'm Madison Miller," and stuck out her free right hand.

James took her hand lightly to shake but was surprised by her grip. She squeezed his hand firmly and shook much more like a guy than a girl. "So, what's up," he asked, as she released his hand.

"War, I guess; though no one seems to be sure."

That definitely shook James. *War* was not a thought that had even entered his mind. A thousand questions seemed to come to him all at once.

"War? With who?" he asked. It didn't really seem at all possible. Oh sure, the U.S. military still maintained bases all over the world, but the war in Afghanistan had ended years ago. War with North Korea had seemed imminent at one time until it became obvious that it was a war no one could ever win.

"Not sure," she said, returning the radio to her ear. "The only thing that's certain right now is that someone has taken out the internet and most, if not all, of our satellite communications."

Chapter 5

The falling snow outside his window reminded James of the scene two and a half years ago when the war had brought the world to a standstill. This was the same window of the same dorm room that he had occupied every school year since he was a freshman here at Colorado One. Now a senior, he would be graduating and leaving Colorado One behind in just two more months. He could see a few vehicles moving up and down Highway 36, but there wasn't nearly as much traffic as there used to be on a Friday afternoon. Another very notable difference was the number of people who were walking along the shoulders of the highway. Some carried packs, and more than a few were pushing or pulling carts or wagons. *More and more every day,* he thought. *The poor who can't afford any other transportation; worse yet, the homeless, who really have nowhere to go.*

The snow seemed to be ending. *Not even enough to cover the ground. Another winter ending like last winter,* he thought. *Another winter with practically no snowpack.* The ongoing drought was really taking a toll now. Even with trainloads of water being freighted in from the Great Lakes, there wouldn't be enough for everyone to get through another summer. He had the thought that many of those down below who were headed north along Highway 36 sensed the same thing and were trying to get someplace where water was plentiful. *Where are they going,* he thought, *Wyoming, Montana, maybe Canada? A long way to push or pull a wagon or a cart.*

It was mid-March and the daytime high temperatures had already been reaching into the eighties here in Boulder. The cold front that had brought this meager snow would be gone by tomorrow, along with any trace of what little moisture it had brought with it. As he watched the poor headed up the highway, James felt the familiar pangs of guilt. What made him so different than them? How was it that he had a brand-new Jeep parked in the seniors parking lot – underclassmen were not allowed vehicles – and so many others had nothing but the clothes on their backs and whatever they could carry with them?

He thought about the Jeep that had been given to him by his father as a birthday present less than a month ago. It was a pure autonomous vehicle; 4-wheel direct electric drive, lightly armored with bullet-proof glass. It would protect him from the random shots that were sometimes fired at the wealthy, as well as keeping him secure from any random crowd he happened to encounter. The Jeep gave him a sense of freedom that he had never had before. He could go wherever he wanted to go, whenever he wanted to go there. *But what happens if the net goes down again? Won't happen*, he thought.

The Great Mid-East war, as it was now being called, had lasted only a few months, but it had changed the world more than anything had since World War II. The culmination of centuries of religious conflict between Sunni and Shia, between Christian and Muslim, and decades of conflict between Iran and Saudi Arabia, and Israelis and Palestinians; the war had brought all of these conflicts to an end. At least, for now. The war had also brought a final end to the age of the American Empire. The entire Middle East was mostly in ruins now; the few people who were left were simply surviving, they didn't have time or energy left over for conflict. What the war had failed to take away, was left to the destruction of climate change. Destruction that was more and more pronounced with every passing year.

It had, of course, been China that had taken down much of the infrastructure of the United States, and just as certainly, the U.S.A. had returned the favor. It may have been known as the Great Mid-East war, but it had been as much of a world war as any of the wars of the twentieth century. A few countries had been able to stay out of the conflict. Most notably, those in Central and South America, and a few in central and southern Africa. Even though they had managed to avoid taking part in the conflict, the war brought profound changes to these countries as well. With the previous world order turned upside down and inside out, these countries now had to depend on themselves and their neighbors. There was no longer a World Bank or an International Monetary Fund. Unburdened by the demands of the previously powerful nations of the world, most of these countries would have been thriving, if not for the disasters of climate change.

Although it didn't seem like it to most of its citizens, the United States had actually come through the conflict in better shape than many other countries. Through a lot of behind the scenes diplomatic efforts and threats of nuclear annihilation, the U.S.A, Russia, and China had managed to keep most of the destruction of the war contained to the Middle-East. Much of its influence over the rest of the world was long gone, but at least the U.S.A. was still an intact sovereign nation. And, to the surprise of many, much of the technology that had helped to temporarily make the U.S.A. the world's only super-power continued to function.

The Defense Department had long been aware of the vulnerabilities of the internet and the satellites that everyone depended on. To compensate for those vulnerabilities, top secret dark projects had been in the works since before the end of the twentieth century. There were redundant satellites to replace those that were taken out by the Chinese; some already in orbit and some ready to launch and activate on a moment's notice. As for the internet, that was also ready to be replaced. The infrastructure was already in place on that fateful day, two and a half years ago, when the world wide web went dark. Unlike the rest of the world that struggled to get the web back up and functioning, the U.S. simply activated its replacement. Something the government called Amerinet. Amerinet worked much like the old internet, except that it was most definitely not world-wide. In fact, in the United States, it was no longer possible to even access the wider internet, except by going through special servers that were operated by the new Cyber Security Administration.

James felt the familiar vibration of the com in his pocket. "Diggy, big screen," he said, without even taking the com out of his pocket. He had renamed his digital assistant Diggy. Assy was just too juvenile, now that he considered himself grown up. He turned away from the window to the big screen above his desk and was surprised to see Madison on screen. He'd been expecting a call from Anna.

"Hi Maddi, you're looking great today!" As he said that, he smiled broadly at the screen. Maddi did look great, but then she always did. James had started dating Madison immediately after their meeting on the day the net went dark. It had been an interesting tightrope walk, keeping up a long-distance romance with Anna, while at the same time actively pursuing Maddi.

"Hi, James," Maddi wasn't smiling. Rather, she had kind of a sad look on her face, and her bright blue eyes didn't seem to sparkle like they usually did. He could tell from the background that she wasn't in her dorm room either.

"Maddi, is something wrong?" He felt a little foolish that he hadn't noticed her demeanor right off the bat.

"Can you come down to the lounge?" It seemed almost like a plea.

"Sure. You want me to come down now?" He was supposed to meet her in the lounge in about an hour for a date.

"Please," she said, "I can't wait another hour."

As he walked down the corridor to the stairwell, James hardly ever used the elevators, he thought about Maddi and their relationship. He had a real sense of foreboding. She had said that she couldn't wait another hour. James had been anxiously looking forward to the evening as well. But he was pretty sure that another night of sneaking Maddi into his room and into his bed wasn't what she had in mind. It was definitely what he had in mind; what he had been looking forward to since the last time, which had been almost two weeks ago.

James and Maddi's relationship had developed slowly at first. He had only seen her a couple of times that first year after the net went down. It had been so chaotic then, with the transition from the internet to Amerinet occupying so much of everyone's time and energy. All classes had been canceled at first, and it was thought that everyone would have to go home. It didn't take long for everyone to realize, however, that no one was going to go anywhere soon. Not with so many autonomous vehicles parked all over the streets and highways, unable to function without the connectivity that they depended on. A national state of emergency had been declared along with the declaration of war, and the military had been given the task of getting the nations' infrastructure back up. Interestingly, the military's communications infrastructure never even seemed to go down. Apparently, the military was much more prepared than most of the experts had thought they were. Most American troops had been brought home from all over the world to tackle the infrastructure problems in the United States. Unlike previous wars, troops weren't really needed. As a matter of fact, they were mostly evacuated. The Great Mid-east war had mostly been about the emptying of American, Russian, and Chinese stockpiles of trillions of dollars' worth of bombs, missiles, and even a few nukes. It wasn't so much a war that had been fought, as it was a region of the world that had been blown up. The war had directly claimed the lives of tens of millions of people, but active military personnel made up a very small fraction of all those killed. Most of those killed and injured were civilians. Millions more had been killed indirectly and were still dying all over the world, as a result of the failures of infrastructure and disruptions of fuels, food, and water.

James was remembering the first time he had sneaked Maddi into his room, as he walked down the first flight of stairs. It had been the previous fall shortly after the start of their senior year. Getting her up to his room without getting caught had all been a matter of a simple disguise. The school had a nice co-ed fitness center and gym located a short walk from the dorm. On that day back in October, James and Maddi had separately gone to the fitness center and then met up there. When Maddi went into the fitness center, she was wearing shorts and a light blue windbreaker with her long hair blowing in the wind. She had been carrying a gym bag that was the schools green and gold colors. Within fifteen minutes of Maddi going into the fitness center – James had arrived before her – James, and what appeared to be another boy emerged. They were both wearing black hooded sweatshirts and sunglasses. James was not wearing the hood up on his sweatshirt, but the other boy had his head totally covered. The two walked briskly to the dorm and just as briskly up the stairs, which were seldom used, as most preferred the elevators. It was only when they were safely inside James' room that Maddi took off her sunglasses at the same time as James pushed the hood off her head and kissed her. It wasn't long before, with a lot of awkward inexperience, they were removing the rest of each other's clothes. Before that day, James had always dreamed of Anna being the first. He still had feelings of guilt about having sex with Maddi instead of saving himself for Anna.

He was just about to the bottom of the last flight of stairs when he felt the com vibrate in his pocket again. *Shit,* he thought. He had forgotten about the expected call From Anna. He stopped at the bottom of the stairs to take the call, hesitated, then decided he would just have to call Anna back.

The lounge was mostly empty. There were a couple of guys that James vaguely recognized playing virtual chess at one of the gaming tables; the holographic pieces seeming to float in the air just above the board. Over in the corner by one of the big picture windows, there was a couple who were obviously engaged in a romantic conversation sitting in one of the love seats that were scattered here and there among the overstuffed chairs that were the main furniture.

Looking around, James spotted Madison over in the other corner of the lounge. She was sitting in one of the big overstuffed chairs, half turned to where she could look out the window at the falling snow. As she turned at his approach, he could see that she was crying.

"What's wrong?" he asked, taking a seat in the chair next to hers. The chairs were arranged so they were seated at about a forty-five-degree angle toward each other, with both having a view out the window while carrying on a face to face conversation at the same time.

There were tears in Maddi's blue eyes, as she looked straight into his and said, "I have to stop seeing you, James."

"Why?" The one-word question betrayed his emotions to the extent that it was like a million questions all at once. Why now? What happened? What did I do? Why me? He could feel the tightening in his throat and feel the sting of tears starting to form in his own eyes.

The tears in Maddi's eyes were drying, a steely resolve replacing the sadness on her features. "I have a boyfriend back home." It was a statement of fact spoken flatly, without emotion. "I'm going home next week, and I don't want to see you anymore."

The statement was like a slap in the face. "What do you mean you're going home next week, graduation isn't until May?"

"I have all of my credits and they're letting me graduate early. I'm going back home to start classes at Stanford. Justin is already enrolled…I'm sorry James."

The finality of the way she said, I'm sorry James, drained most of his sadness away, as it was replaced by jealousy. No, not jealousy really; it was more simple anger. The strange thing was, he wasn't really angry at Madison, he was angry at himself. Angry that he had let himself fall for Maddi when the feelings he had for Anna were stronger than anything he had ever felt for the blue-eyed, strawberry blonde from California.

He stood up, the tears in his eyes mostly stopped and the tightness in his throat relaxing. "Fine," he said. "Just so you know, I have a girlfriend, too." He turned and walked away. It was the last time James ever saw or heard from Madison Miller.

On his way back up to his room, James wasn't thinking about Madison, he was thinking about Anna. He was trying to decide if he should tell Anna about Maddi. Maybe that would clear his conscience, but he didn't really have anything to feel guilty about. He had never lied to Anna, except maybe by omission; and they had never talked about not dating other people. For all he knew, Anna had been dating someone else, too. That thought stopped him in his tracks. As he resumed walking, he wondered…for all he knew, Anna might be having sex with another boy. Hell, she might have had sex with lots of boys. Now there was a thought that brought out actual jealousy, whether it was warranted or not. By the time he got to his room, he had worked up an overwhelming desire to see Anna. Not just on the comscreen, but to really see her in person; to actually be with her.

"Diggy, call Anna." He was taking clothes out of the dresser drawer and putting them in his overnight bag when Anna's face came on screen. "Anna, I'm coming out to Kremmling to see you." He hardly even looked up from packing.

"What? When?" The look on her face was definitely one of surprise, but James wasn't sure, as he looked up at the screen, whether it was a pleasant surprise, or not.

"I'll leave early and be there first thing in the morning. If the roads are good, that is."

"James, wait…how can you come here? I thought your Dad wouldn't let you."

"He won't, but he doesn't have to know." James' thoughts were in overdrive now. Since he had the new Jeep, James usually drove down home to Castle Pines on the weekends, but he had already told his Mom and Dad that he was going to stay at school this weekend to study. He hadn't bothered to tell them that what he planned on studying was the anatomy of a certain girl from Southern California. "I already told them that I'm not coming home this weekend. They'll think I'm just studying here at school."

"James…James, wait a minute. You can't drive out here early in the morning. It's been snowing in the mountains all day long. Are the passes even open?"

He looked up from the overnight bag at Anna's face on the big screen, not sure about the expression he saw on her dark features; not sure what was written in those deep brown eyes. "Anna, don't you want to see me?" The hurt in his voice was unmistakable.

Anna's beautiful dark eyes softened and lit up. "Oh James, I do want to see you," she said. "More than anything. It's just that I wish you'd let me know sooner. Why don't you wait until next weekend? You can drive out Friday afternoon, and we can spend the whole weekend together."

Reluctantly, James had agreed to wait until the following weekend to go to Kremmling. After hanging up, though, he had changed his mind. Anna wanted to see him as much as he wanted to see her, he was sure of that. He'd decided that he'd just have to surprise her.

Anna was right about the snow in the mountains. The snow in Boulder, however, had stopped sometime shortly after dark. There was still no light in the east as James unplugged the charger from his Jeep. Anticipation had kept him from sleeping well, which was very odd for James Mendez. He usually slept like a log. At times, the com alarm even had trouble waking him up. This morning, he had bounded out of bed at four o'clock, even though the com was set for five.

It's gonna be warm today, he thought. There was a warm chinook breeze already pushing the cold front off to the east. The sky was brilliantly clear, millions of stars like tiny jewels shimmering in the pre-dawn darkness. It wasn't deep dark, the moon was nearly full, but it was just about to set behind the mountains to the west. *Follow that moon*, he thought, as he settled into the autonomous jeep. Instead, he just said, "Nav, take us to the BR Ranch near Kremmling."

James watched, as the map appeared on the screen in front of him. It was centered on Kremlin, Montana, and seemed to be searching for the BR Ranch. "Not Kremlin, Montana; Kremm-ling Colorado". He said, emphasizing the G at the end of Kremmling. The map re-centered instantly on the town of Kremmling, and then a marker pin appeared, looking like some kind of giant pole rising right up out of the location of the BR ranch headquarters about halfway between Kremmling and Silverthorne.

A female voice with a slight British accent came out of a hidden speaker. "Is this the correct destination?" she asked.

"Yes," James said. *Maybe I'll try another voice*, he thought. The British accent had seemed cute when he set it up, but for some reason, he now found it kind of annoying.

The Jeep backed nearly silently out of the parking spot and pulled out onto Highway 36. "There is a delay near the Eisenhower-Johnson Tunnel," the British voice said, "but it is still our quickest route. We should reach our destination by eight-fifteen."

James adjusted the seat to a full reclining position and closed his eyes. "Diggy, wake me up at seven-thirty, and don't let the queen of England disturb me unless it's an emergency."

This time, the answer that came out of the hidden speaker was the familiar voice of his digital assistant. "If the queen of England calls, I'll tell her you are not to be disturbed."

James had to laugh. "Yeah, and don't let the nav-system wake me up, either."

They weren't moving. James pushed the button that raised him up out of his reclined position. It was bright sunlight shining through the bullet-proof glass of the Jeep. He could see that they were somewhere high in the mountains. Snow banks still lined both sides of I-70, but the banks of snow were only about a quarter of what they used to be this time of year. *The snow's going to be all gone in another month*, he thought. *It'll be a long dry summer if the snowpack's already gone by April.* He looked at the nav-screen and found that they were sitting on I-70 about two miles from the tunnel's east portal. The clock on the screen said 7:03. They must have been sitting stationary for quite a while; he had definitely caught some sleep. The Jeep was in the left lane; on the right, there was an autonomous electric semi blocking his view. In front, there was a single SUV and then just empty highway. *Looks like a new Benz*, he thought. Turning to look back, directly behind there was one of the newer autonomous electric buses that were, to a large extent, replacing the electric passenger trains. The buses were now the primary mode of transportation for the masses. At least, for those who could afford a ticket. Over on the eastbound lanes, traffic, what traffic there was, seemed to be moving normally. There wasn't much traffic at all, just a few semis. The only other private transportation that James saw was the Benz parked in front of him.

"Nav, why are we stopped?" There didn't seem to be any obstructions in front of the Benz. There was a red stoplight, presumably there just in case a human driver happened along in an antique vehicle.

"There is a snow removal operation in progress," the Brit voice said. "The delay should last for approximately two more hours, our ETA at the BR Ranch is now ten-twenty."

Two more hours? James thought. *How can it take two hours to open up the highway?* "Can't we just go over the pass?" he asked the Nav, referring to the old Highway 6 route over Loveland Pass.

"Loveland Pass is closed, with no planned reopening," was the reply from the navigation unit.

"Diggy, call Anna." James couldn't remember ever calling Anna this early, but he had to let her know he was on his way to see her. He had awakened with the beginnings of a new plan in mind.

"James?" Anna's voice came out of the Jeep's sound system.

"Good morning." He noticed right away that Anna had answered voice only, apparently, she wasn't prepared for James to see her yet. *Like I wouldn't think she was beautiful without makeup,* he thought. "Guess where I am?"

"Umm, how am I supposed to know? Let's see; did you go home after all?"

"I'm waiting on snow removal sitting here on I-70. I should be there by about ten-thirty."

There was a long silence before Anna spoke. "You're coming here - today? I thought we'd decided on next weekend." Definitely surprise in her voice, but, once again, James wasn't really sure that it seemed like a pleasant surprise. "Does your Grandpa know?"

"Nobody knows but you. As a matter of fact, I have an idea – let's not let anyone else know at all. I'm only coming out there to see you, not Grandpa."

"And how are you going to show up at the ranch without Chuck knowing you're here?" She was at least now sounding a little bit intrigued.

"Is it warm enough that you can take Pintada out for a ride, by yourself?"

"Yes, the weather is beautiful, but I can't take Pintada anywhere. She has a new colt. Remember? I told you she was pregnant."

"Oh yeah," now he remembered. "What about Midnight? You said you'd been riding him some, just to keep him in shape."

"Yeah – I suppose I could take Midnight out for a ride this morning, but James..." She didn't get a chance to finish.

James didn't let her finish, all he heard was the part about she could take Midnight for a ride. "You remember that old forest road a half mile or so south of the south pasture? How 'bout I meet you there?"

There was another pause on the line, before she answered, more than a little frustration creeping into her voice. "I haven't been on that road for a long time, James. I'm not sure it's even passable."

"Surely I can get at least a little way off of Highway 9. We can meet about a quarter of a mile in. That way my jeep won't be visible from the highway." He felt the Jeep start to move just as he said it.

"James, I wish you would have let me know sooner. I have a" there was a pause, "I had plans to go into town today."

Oblivious to the undertones of frustration and disappointment in her voice, all James heard was that she'd *had* plans to go into town. Which to him meant only that her plans could now be changed. "I couldn't let you know sooner, I just decided last night. Anna, I need to see you. What do you want me to do, just turn around and go home?"

There was a silence and a barely audible sigh before she answered. "No James, I do want to see you. I really do. I can get out of going to town." Then, in a happier sounding voice, "How soon did you say you'd be here?"

After the conversation ended, Anna sat on the edge of her bed, looking at the picture on the home screen of her com. It was a picture of her and James sitting side by side on Pintada and Midnight. Just another picture of two happy kids, seemingly, without a care in the world. She sat that way for a few minutes before telling her com to call Will. Will wasn't going to like her breaking their date, but deep down she knew that, even though she'd dated him for almost a year, Will had never been anything but a surrogate. She may have given in to physical need and given her virginity to Will, but that twelve-year-old girl in the picture on her com had already known she was in love, way back then.

Having slept most of the way from Boulder, James hadn't noticed the condition of I-70. It had been seven years since he had traveled over the mountains. Maintenance on the old highway wasn't what it used to be. *Good thing it doesn't have to carry the traffic that it once did*, he thought, as barriers narrowed the road down to one lane. The left lane was just gone. A large hole had opened up and half of I-70 had slid down the mountain. He wondered if it would ever be repaired. *Probably not unless this lane goes, too*. It wasn't a very comforting thought, as they passed the gaping hole.

As bad as it was, Interstate 70 proved to be in much better shape than Highway 9 leading from Silverthorne to Kremmling. Being the major east-west corridor for truck freight, I-70 did get some maintenance, but Highway 9, in recent years, was mostly used by just a few farmers and ranchers; and the school buses that carried their children to school in Kremmling or Silverthorne. The potholes and cracked and missing asphalt made it quite an obstacle course for the Jeep's navigation system. As they got to within a few miles of the BR, James had the sudden realization that the nav system was taking him directly to the ranch. For all he knew, it might not even have the old forest road in its database.

"Nav, I want to change our destination, show me an aerial map of this area." It took some study for James to re-orient the lay of the land with his memory. He zoomed in on the BR and struggled to remember all of the places he and Anna had been six years ago. It was easy to make out the buildings that comprised the ranch headquarters. From there, he could easily make out the big meadow to the north. He studied the area on the south side of Spider Creek. The south pasture wasn't nearly as easy to distinguish as the big meadow on the north side of the ranch. It wasn't nearly as big, and much of the terrain of the south pasture looked like the rest of the surrounding area. Finally, though, he spotted the forest road he was looking for. He zoomed in to where the map was large enough for him to touch the spot where the forest road left Highway 3. "This is our new destination," he said. "I want to turn off on this road and stop about a quarter of a mile From Highway 3."

"I am sorry," the British voice said, in a matter of fact manner, "the road you have selected is not in my database."

"I want to go there, anyway. At least get me to the intersection. And change your voice." The accent was suddenly very irritating. "Use the voice of an American man."

"Certainly," the voice was now a man's voice, with no noticeable accent at all. "Our ETA at the intersection is ten thirty-two."

As it turned out, the forest road was completely impassable by vehicle. A large dead aspen tree had fallen across the old road no more than twenty yards from the highway. James had the Jeep back up into the forest road as far as the log and parked it there. Not that getting off of the highway was very important; James had only seen two other vehicles on the road this side of Silverthorne. There were several more fallen logs that he had to go over and around, as he walked up the road. The feelings of anticipation hadn't subsided, but, as he approached the rendezvous, strong feelings of nervousness were taking over. Now that he was this close, doubts started creeping in. Did Anna want to see him, as much as he wanted to see her? What was it that he felt for Anna? Was this true love? He knew that what he had felt for Maddi wasn't love. It had definitely been lust, but it wasn't love. What did sex have to do with love, anyway? If he was truly in love with Anna, and if she was in love with him, would sex change the feelings they had for each other?

He saw Midnight first, but not before Midnight saw him. James came around a bend in the old forest road to find the horse staring straight at him from the shadows of an aspen grove. Midnight's ears were following James' movements as well, and his nostrils were searching the air to ascertain what, or who, it was walking up the forest road.

At first, he didn't see Anna. She was sitting on a fallen aspen at the edge of a small clearing off to the side of where she had tied Midnight to a tree. The hopes and fears that Anna had been feeling, as she waited for James were, if anything, even stronger than the emotions he had been feeling. Seeing him come into view was terrifying and thrilling at the same time. She wanted to run into his arms, at the same time she was afraid to. She wanted nothing more than she wanted to make love to this love of her life. She was also terrified that the act of physical love would diminish or destroy their love for each other.

Anna stood. She started walking toward James. He continued walking toward her. Neither said a word. They came together in the middle of the clearing; their eyes were locked in a silent embrace before they wrapped their arms around each other as their lips met. At that moment, it seemed they had always been together; that they would always be together. Eternity was fully contained in that one moment of holding onto each other, expressing infinite feelings with their kiss.

They made love on a bed of aspen leaves, in the middle of a clearing, in the middle of nowhere. It was paradise. It was heaven on earth. They were, for those fleeting few minutes, at the center of their own universe. They might as well have been the only two people on earth.

The afternoon was gone in an instant. With their clothes back on, James and Anna sat together on the same fallen tree that Anna had been sitting on when James arrived. James had his arm around Anna, and she had her face snuggled against his chest.

"I don't want you to go," she said. There were tears in her eyes; tears of happiness. "I love you, James."

"I love you too, Anna. More than anything. I'll be back before you know it. How could I ever stay away?"

Chapter 6

The trip back to Boulder had been mostly a blur, with nothing at all worth remembering. James had grabbed a burger in Silverthorne while the Jeep was recharging. He had then slept most of the way to Boulder. He had even slept through the long delay near the west portal of the tunnel.

It was almost four o'clock when the Jeep pulled onto the charging pad at the dorm, and James made his way up to his room. His first thought on entering was that he had left the light on. Then he saw Don sitting in the recliner looking at him.

"Hello James," It was a friendly greeting like they'd just ran into each other on the street somewhere.

"Don, what are you doing here?" An almost imperceptible shiver seemed to run up James' spine.

What the hell was Don doing here? He looked at the man sitting relaxed in the reclincr. Don always appeared relaxed. He wasn't that much older than James, only in his late twenties, and he and James were about the same size and build. James worked out enough to be well muscled, but nothing like Don. Don's muscles were like steel springs, always tight; and yet, paradoxically, always relaxed. Like the springs of a cocked bear trap, full of tension contained in a misleadingly relaxed pose by the trap's trip mechanism. Don was, among other things, highly trained in self-defense, and James knew that he was also always armed. Don was his father's favorite bodyguard. Strange as it seemed, he was also James' favorite of those who were tasked with protecting the Mendez family. James and Don had always had a rapport that James didn't ever feel around the others. Maybe it was the fact that Don was much closer to his age, or maybe it was just that Robert had tasked Don with protecting his son much more than he had any of the other security personnel. As a result, James had spent much more time with Don than he had with the small army of security that worked for Robert Mendez.

Don smiled. "Well, James, I'm here on orders; your dad sent me." His smile widened a little more. "Course you probably already figured that. Fact is, it's time to go."

James looked at him blankly. *Time to go? Time to go where?* It was then that he noticed that his things were gone. The desk was bare, the picture of Anna was gone from the nightstand by the bed. As he looked around, he could see through the open closet door that even his clothes were gone.

"What do you mean time to go? Graduation is still over a month away."

"Guess you graduated early. Robert wants to see you, in his words, as soon as possible."

He knew. Somehow, he knew I went to see Anna. The thought was accompanied by a cascade of emotions. There was a bit of fear, along with dread at the confrontation with his father that was now imminent. But mostly, he felt anger. His father had been spying on him or at least tracking his movements. *How? How had he known?* More importantly, *why? Why had his own father been spying on him? What gave him the right? I'm eighteen years old,* he thought. *I'm an adult. I don't have to do what I'm told.*

"Tell him no. You tell him I don't want to see him, and I want him to stop spying on me. I'm not a kid anymore." The anger was boiling over now. "Never mind, I'll tell him. Assie…" in the heat of the moment he reverted back to his digital assistant's old name, before correcting himself, which only added to the level of frustration. "Diggy, call Dad."

"He won't answer." Don still seemed totally relaxed in the recliner. "You know that. If he was going to simply request your presence, he would have called you."

As the com continued to ring, James knew that Don was right. If his father had meant to simply request his presence, he would have called. Robert Mendez was not much in the habit of making requests. He was much more in the habit of simply giving orders. Orders that were not to be ignored.

"Diggy, stop the call. And what if I refuse to go with you? What are you going to do, kidnap me?" The edge was going off his anger. He was still mad as hell at his Dad, but not at Don.

The expression on Don's face turned cold. He looked at James with an icy stare. "That's not something you want to do James. Look around. All your stuff's already gone. The school won't let you stay, and I'm taking the Jeep when I go. The Jeep's going to Castle Pines, whether you're in it or not."

James broke away from Don's icy stare. The blinds were open, he looked out at the darkness of night. Somewhere in the open land off to the northeast, he could see the flickering glow of distant campfires. *What am I going to do,* he thought? *Join the homeless out there?* Suddenly, the anger was gone. In its place was the beginnings of a plan. "Let's go," he said, as he turned and headed back out the door, without even looking back at Don.

The short trip from Boulder down Highway 36 to Denver was totally unlike any trip that James had ever been on with Don. Neither spoke hardly a word. As soon as they were on the road, Don was on his com texting. James presumed that the messaging was to his father and Don didn't want James to hear a voice conversation. His suspicion was confirmed when Don redirected the Jeep's Nav to take them to the MICI office building downtown. The MICI, which stood for Mendez Investment and Consulting, Inc., was a somewhat unassuming office building in downtown Denver. Other than the security guards and the armor gated entrance to the below-ground parking area, the thirty-story building was much like the other office buildings in downtown Denver. Few people knew that it was the world headquarters for a multi-billion-dollar empire. A financial empire that Robert James Mendez had built from the ground up.

The clock on the nav screen showed 5:03 as the Jeep pulled off of 20th into the drive that led to the underground parking. The guardhouse at the gate was manned twenty-four hours a day. No electronic enabled entrance gate for Robert Mendez. That would never have been secure enough to suit him. As a matter of fact, the gate, as well as the rest of the building's security measures were not connected to Amerinet at all. Anything connected could be hacked.

"Kind of early for Dad to be at work, isn't it?" James asked, finally breaking the silence between them.

"Yeah, it is. I'm not even sure he's here, but this is where he said to bring you."

The guard stepped out of the guardhouse armed with an M4 rifle and stepped up to the Jeep's window. James knew that there were at least two other armed guards stationed in armored rooms, where the two windows above the opening to the underground parking looked down on the drive. Those two windows were one-way bullet-proof glass with openings between them where heavier armaments like armor-piercing rockets could be fired on anything that was sitting in the driveway below.

Don rolled down the window of the Jeep. "Howdy Mike," he said. "How's it hangin'?"

"Don! didn't expect to see you. What? You lowering your standards, riding around in a plain old Jeep?" It was obvious that the guard felt subordinate to Don, and then he leaned in to see James. "And James!" he really didn't expect to see James Mendez. Now Mike was all business. "I'll open the gate."

"Hey Mike, is the boss up there?" Don asked as the guard turned back toward the gate.

"Not sure, but I think so. An airdrone landed up on the pad about fifteen minutes ago. Since nobody bothered to shoot it down, I figure it was him."

The entire top floor of the MICI Building was Robert Mendez' private suite. Totally self-contained, he could stay here full time if he so desired. The elevator that James and Don rode up from the parking garage opened into a reception area where Margie, Robert's personal assistant, would have been seated at her desk during business hours. The semi-circular desk was empty at this late hour, but the door to Robert's office behind the desk was half-way open.

"James, please come in." Robert's voice came over the intercom as soon as James and Don stepped from the elevator. "Don, thanks as always. Please relax in the lounge for a while, if you would."

Don immediately headed down the wide hallway toward the lounge. James, feeling strong trepidation and wishing he were most anywhere else, nonetheless, walked purposefully through the door into his father's office.

Robert Mendez was seated behind the L shaped mahogany desk, but he was turned away from the desk, looking out the huge corner windows at the lights of downtown Denver. He was not a large man. James was a couple of inches taller than his father and had a huskier build. Robert was dressed as he always was, in a tailored grey silk suit. Clean shaven, with his black hair immaculately in place, the only thing missing this late in the evening was his necktie. Otherwise, he looked the same as he always did at work. Right down to the cup of coffee that he held in his right hand. For some reason, the coffee caught James' attention more than anything else. He had the thought that he seldom saw his father without a cup of coffee. For that matter, it seemed like years since he had seen him dressed in something other than a suit.

"James, come in and sit down." Robert didn't even turn to look at his son, just continued looking out the window.

"Okay, Dad. I don't seem to have much choice, do I?" He walked across the plush carpet and sat in one of the chairs across the desk from his father.

Robert finally turned to look at his son. He set the coffee cup down on the desk without taking his eyes off of James. He didn't say anything for a long moment, just looked at his son with what seemed like a longing for something. "Choices," he said. The one word just hung there. "I guess that's why we're here, isn't it? It's all a matter of choices."

"I didn't choose to be here, Dad. Don didn't really give me a choice."

A kind of sad smile came over Robert's features. "In many ways, I didn't choose to be here, either, son. But the choices we've made definitely brought us to this place and time." He swept his left hand through the air, indicating the place they were in. The smile left his face, but the sadness remained. "I guess it's past time for us to talk about the choices I've made in my life. And, more importantly, the choices you have to make in yours."

"I'm beginning to wonder if I really have any choices in my life Dad." Anger was starting to come back to James. "You seem to be making my choices for me."

Robert looked away, his focus seeming to shift off into the distance somewhere. "Maybe none of us have any choice," his voice was soft. He seemed to be speaking more to that distance than to James. Abruptly, he refocused on James, and a strong tone of command returned to his voice. "Have you ever wondered why I never speak of my youth? Or, how I got to be where I am? Have you ever wondered about how I came to marry your mother?"

James hadn't wondered about any of those things. There was no need to wonder. Like anyone else who was as rich and powerful as his father, Robert Mendez' life was an open book, in news and magazine articles, as well as in Wikipedia. Anyone could find out anything they wanted to about Robert Mendez, or so it had always seemed to James. His was the quintessential story of the American dream. Robert's parents had immigrated to the United States from Guatemala in the early 1990s. Unfortunately for them, they had done so illegally. Fortunately for Robert, he was born in Pueblo, Colorado, which made him a U.S. citizen. His father worked as a laborer in the construction industry, while his mother worked at whatever odd jobs she could find. In short, Robert Mendez' parents did whatever they could find to do, just to survive and to provide for Robert and Robert's older sister, Marie.

"Everybody knows your story, Dad. You're famous. What's to wonder?"

"Yes, everybody knows my story," his gaze seemed to wander off into the distance again. "How I was able to overcome the deportation of my family and everything else to become the self-made billionaire that I am today." He looked at James and smiled again. "It's a good story. A good story with a lot of holes. Yes, I was able to work my way through school to learn economics and finance. But the story doesn't say why I chose to study those subjects. Do you know why, James?"

"I guess that was what you were interested in."

"But why?" there was a new intensity in Robert's voice. "Why was I interested in finance? Why was that the choice I made."

In spite of himself, James was now curious. *What was his father leading up to? What was this really all about?* "I don't know. What made you interested in finance? Did you actually control what you were interested in? Seems to me that we don't really control what interests us, only what we do with those interests."

"Exactly!" Robert proclaimed. "I wasn't interested in economics and finance at all. People think I'm a financial genius. I'm not a financial genius. My interest was in power. Pure and simple. When my family was deported, and I was left alone I was the same age as you are now. At first, I was interested in law. After all, it was the law and the people that made the laws that had deported them. At first, I thought that power was in the law and that I should study law and learn to wield that power. But power isn't in the law, James. Money is power. That's what I was really after. If you have enough money, you can control the laws. Without money, legal knowledge will get you nowhere."

James was fascinated, his father had never, in his eighteen years of life, talked to him like this. He had always been rather stern. He hadn't been exactly cold to James, but he wasn't exactly warm, either. He had mostly just seemed distant. James had always, in his own mind, blamed that distance on the fact that Robert's parents and sister had all been murdered shortly after they were sent back to Guatemala. Now, it seemed there was more to it than that.

"So, you decided to study finance to acquire money?" James asked, his growing interest in his father's story obvious.

"No! Not to acquire money, to acquire power. Money is just a vehicle. A means to an end, nothing more." He seemed to grow introspective, and then, in a softer voice, "there is never enough. You can never control everything. No matter how much money and power, you just can't control everything." Once again, he looked off into some unknown distance, leaving James to wonder where his mind was going.

"Is that why you have been spying on me? Are you trying to control me, too? Is that why you have kept me away from Grandpa's ranch?" The feelings James had when he realized his father had been spying on him had morphed from burning hot anger to a cold slow simmering resentment.

Robert turned and looked at James again. He had a sad smile on his face. "No son, I haven't been trying to keep you away from Chuck or the ranch. The Duran girl is the problem."

"What do you mean, problem? Anna's not a problem. I love Anna. You can't keep me away from her anymore. I'm going to go live with Grandpa Chuck. I'm eighteen years old and you can't stop me." James' plan had come into focus. He would simply go live at the BR. He could be with Anna every day. He could learn how to be a rancher and help Grandpa Chuck. His grandfather was getting old and probably needed the help anyway.

The sad smile left his father's face, and his eyes turned cold. "I won't allow it. I won't allow you to throw away what I have built. You will go to Harvard or Yale and learn to take over what I have built. And you will meet someone who is worthy of you to make you forget about Anna. I had hoped that Madison

Miller girl would have done it, she's from a good family. A family with power. The kind of family that can add to what I've built. Oh well, there will be others. You will find the right girl at college, just like I found your mother."

Anger welled up again in James. Anger, defiance, and righteous indignation. "Like hell, I will!" He stood up and turned to leave.

"James, if you walk out that door, there won't be any coming back." His father's voice was cold and menacing. "You, Chuck, and the entire Duran family will end up cold and homeless, just like all the rest."

It was a threat. James was half-way to the door when it hit him. It was not an idle threat; the threat was very real. Could his father actually somehow force Grandpa Chuck and the Duran family off of the BR Ranch. As impossible as it seemed, he knew the answer was yes. Robert Mendez probably had the power to make that happen, or did he? He turned back to face his father. At that moment, the only emotion that could describe what he felt toward the man was hatred. He had a sudden realization about his father and mother.

"Did you ever love my mother," he asked, his expression and voice now as cold and hard as his father's. "For that matter, have you ever loved anyone?"

"I love you, son. Your mother may have been a means to an end, but then she gave me you. I love her for that, at least. I love her for giving me you."

"You say you love me, and yet you could throw me to the wolves? Along with Grandpa Chuck? That's a strange way to show love if you ask me."

"I suppose it is, but I won't have you ending up married to a nobody. Squandering away the power that has taken me a lifetime to build. The Mendez family won't ever go backward. If you won't honor your responsibility to all I've built, it'll pass on to someone who will."

Who? James thought. *I'm his only son. Who could he possibly leave all this to?* Then it dawned on him – *why should I care? I don't want to be like him, anyway. Besides, he has no one else.* "You're bluffing," he said, with more confidence than he felt. "I'm all you've got."

The coldness in Robert Mendez' voice was chilling. "You have a cousin, James. He lives in the squalor of Guatemala. There is nothing he would like more than to come to America. To inherit this." He held out his hands as if to encompass the whole world. "He would be grateful. He would know how important it is to gather and maintain power. He would know that there is never enough."

James was shocked to his core. He didn't know the man sitting at the desk. The man who was his father. "How?" he finally said. "How can I have a cousin? Your family was murdered."

"Yes, my family was murdered. The whole world knows that. What no one knows is that I had an older brother who was left behind when my family came to America. He, too, was murdered eventually, but not before he produced a son. I have secretly nurtured and protected my nephew, just as I have nurtured and protected you. So, you see James, it is up to you. You are right, I won't stop you if you decide to throw all of this away, but know this - you won't be ruining your life only. You will also be destroying the life of that girl you say you love. Believe me, I will see to that."

They looked at each other for a long quiet moment. James trying to understand how, after eighteen years, he could know so little of his father. *How can I even be his son?*

"Go." Robert broke the moment. "Go and decide. You're right. You're a man now. Your life is yours to decide." He turned back toward the window, and James knew there was nothing left to say. He turned and left the office. His father, who had always been distant, was now a total stranger.

Don was sitting alone in the lounge. Daylight was starting to come through the picture window, where Denver was slowly coming to life at the start of a new day. The windows in the lounge faced to the west, and James could see that sunlight had just reached the tops of the peaks; a warm golden glow, on those snow-capped mountains to the west. His thoughts weren't on the peaks, though. His thoughts were on the Blue River Ranch, off to the west of the peaks. When Don brought him here, he had every intention of telling his father that he was leaving to go live with Grandpa Chuck. Now, he didn't know what to do.

"Am I free to go now?" he said, knowing that Don would already have instructions from his father.

Don didn't look at all surprised by the question. "Yes sir. The boss says I am to return the Jeep. I'm not even supposed to go with you. Looks like you are on your own". He paused, unsure of what to say. "James…I'm sorry."

James wondered how much Don knew, but it really didn't matter. Don may have seemed somewhat like a friend, but that was before. In his other life, the one before today, James had friends. Now, he found himself alone. As the day dawned, he was awakening not to a new day, but to an entirely different world than the one he thought he knew. "Is the Jeep still programmed to my bios then?"

"Of course." There was not a hint of sarcasm in Don's voice. "It's your Jeep."

James glanced through the window at the mountains to the west which were now entirely lit up by the rising sun. The sky was clear except for a few clouds nestled around the top of some of the peaks. He turned and started to leave.

"James," - he stopped. "Be careful out there."

Without so much as even a backward glance, James walked through the door and headed to the parking garage.

"Nav, take me home." His mind in so much turmoil that only part of his thoughts seemed like his own, he was lost in his own head. One basic question kept rolling through his mind in different forms, *what to do? What should I do now? What can I do?* It was never, *what do I want to do?* That was a question he could no longer ask himself. The question of what he wanted to do was no longer relevant. It had been ripped from him by the revelation of who, or what, his father really was.

The number of people on the streets of Denver this early in the morning was astounding. It was obvious that most, if not all, were homeless. Some were wearing little more than rags, while others were dressed quite well. *Newer to the street*, James thought. They were there in droves, going through dumpsters, searching everywhere for any scrap of anything they could find to eat. He remembered something from his childhood as he passed the starving hoards. Back then, it had seemed like every street corner had a resident homeless person with a sign begging for help. This memory was of one incident, in particular. He had been riding somewhere with his mom and dad; must have been five or six years old. They were stopped at a red light, and on the corner next to them, there was a woman dressed in rags with a sign asking for help. He couldn't remember what the sign said. What he did remember was the baby she had strapped to her breast in one of those packs that allows the child to be in front; as opposed to the pictures he'd seen of Native American women with babies strapped to their backs. He remembered his mother had wanted to open the window and give the woman some money. His father had said no. James knew that Robert Mendez hadn't been nearly as wealthy then as he was now, but they had certainly been wealthy enough. As he remembered the scene, he thought he could remember his father saying something like, *We don't give, we take. That's the difference between those who have and those who don't.* Looking back on it now, James wondered if the memory was real, or if he had just manufactured the memory in response to the meeting he'd just come from.

"James! - what are you doing here?" his mother's genuine surprise let him know that she knew nothing of his father's actions. "What's wrong?" she asked, the concern in her voice was reflected in her eyes, as she crossed the room to give her son a hug.

He accepted the hug and held on, grasping for a return to the innocence that had been taken from him. *She doesn't know him any better than I did*, he thought. The thought filled him with sadness. He broke away from his mother. "Why don't you ever go home?" he asked.

The question obviously surprised her. She seemed a bit startled, but then answered simply, "This is my home."

James looked at his mother, searching; trying to see what he may have never seen before. Trying to see, simply by looking at her, what had brought her, and therefore him, to this place in time. Noni Mendez was an attractive woman. She had auburn red hair and blue-green eyes. She was tall for a woman, nearly six feet tall. James had finally grown taller than her only after starting high school. Though his father wasn't there, standing next to her, he knew that she was a little bit taller than him. Noni Pierson had to have grown up wearing cowboy boots. It occurred to him that his mother must have worn boots while growing up on the BR. Everyone who lived there wore boots, almost exclusively. When she became Noni Mendez, the boots became a thing of the past. *His father wouldn't allow it*, he thought. *He would appear short if his beautiful wife was standing next to him in high-heeled boots. Or shoes, for that matter.* He realized he had never seen her in high heels either.

"Don't you ever miss it?" he asked, knowing that she did; knowing that she had to long for her childhood on the old Blue River Ranch.

Noni didn't have to wonder what James was asking if she missed. She thought about all she had lost every day, but she didn't want her son to know. She had played the part far too long to stop now. "Miss what, James?" she asked, looking truly puzzled.

For James, that may have been the saddest moment of that entire evening. The moment when he knew his mother was living a lie. Deep down, he had always known his father was manipulative and power hungry, but the extent of that megalomania had only become clear that night. The sadness of the fact that his mother was being kept from her father and her childhood home, now that he knew the truth, was overwhelming.

"Why, Mother? Do you love Dad that much, that you'd let him keep you from Grandpa?" even as he asked, he knew that was not the case. He knew with a certainty that there was no love left between his mother and his father. As he watched her face crumple and the tears form in her eyes, he felt lost. *Who were these people?* The parents he had looked up to and tried to please his entire life. *How could he not have known how terrible his father really was? How could he not have known that his mother had spent her entire married life subjugating her will to that of his father?*

Seeing that he wouldn't get any answers from his mother, who was now sobbing and covering her face with her hands; he started toward his room to gather his things. "I'm leaving," he said. "I'm going to live with Grandpa."

"No!" he hadn't taken three steps when the exclamation hit him in the back. "James - you don't – you don't understand." The words came hard, between the sobs. "You can't! He won't let you."

"He can't stop me, Mother. I'm eighteen years old, I can do whatever I want."

He heard the sobbing stop and the coldness that came into his mother's voice. "He'll destroy you both."

He turned back to his mother. Her face was now streaked with mascara. She had stopped sobbing as suddenly as she had started. There were no more tears coursing down her cheeks, her lips were set in a firm line and there was a vacant stare in her pretty eyes. "How Mother? How could he possibly make my life any worse?"

Her eyes, that had always provided solace, now stared right past her son, seeing something from another place, or maybe another time. "He'll take the ranch." It was a flat statement, there was no longer any emotion at all in her voice.

James was taken aback. For the second time today, he heard the threat that his father would take away his grandfather's ranch. Land that had belonged to the Pierson family for over a hundred years. "That's crazy mother! Dad doesn't own the BR, Grandpa does. Dad may be rich, but he can't take what doesn't belong to him."

"He controls the oil and gas. He doesn't need a deed to own the BR. All he has to do is shut off the rest of the gas. The land hasn't supported itself for decades. It's the mineral rights that have allowed Dad to live all these years, not the cattle. And besides, he'll take the cattle, too."

Noni Mendez, once a woman who dreamed of a life for her son that was free of her husband's manipulations, slumped into a chair, once again covering her face with her hands. "I'm sorry, James. I am so sorry." Barely above a whisper, the words rang loudly in James' ears as he left the room.

He pulled the com out of his pocket and sat at the desk in his room. He unfolded the com and stared at the picture of Anna that was his home screen. His stare was almost as blank as his mother's had been. He thought about how he had hidden the picture of Anna while dating Madison. He didn't feel shame, it was just a thought. Emotions had left him. Now, there were only thoughts and memories that were almost random. "Diggy, delete the pics of Anna." He couldn't stand to look at her picture now; no more than he could stand to call her and hear her voice. Picking up the com, he pulled up a keyboard and started thumb typing. Dictation would never do. He could no more stand to dictate the words he was typing than he could stand to speak them to her. Instead, he started typing: *My Dearest Anna, I can't see you anymore. I can't explain. You have to forget about me, about us. I can give you nothing but misery, and more than anything else in this life, I want you to be happy.* He looked at the words he'd written for a long time before hitting the send button. "Diggy, block all communications from Anna," he said, as he slumped in his chair and covered his face with his hands, feeling the warm tears flowing freely down his cheeks.

Chapter 7

"Damn it, Steve, this is the third one. What the hell am I supposed to do?"

Sheriff Steve Larson looked up at the grizzled old rancher, whom he'd known as long as he could remember.

"Well Chuck, I know it ain't much consolation, but you're not the only one losing stock these days. Wish I knew what the hell any of us is supposed to do."

Chuck Pierson reached up with his left hand, still holding the reins, and pulled the battered old straw hat off his head. He wiped the sweat off his mostly bald head with a huge right hand and replaced the straw hat over what was left of his once jet-black hair. The black hair had about as much gray now as it did black. That and the weathered wrinkles at the corners of his dark brown eyes gave away the old cowboys age. The sparkle of life that was still in those old brown eyes and the tall muscular build attested to the fact that he was aging well.

"It was probably one of those families of refugees coming up from Texas" the sheriff continued. "Some of 'em are so hungry looking they could probably eat that calf raw."

Chuck looked back at the remains of the calf lying in the trampled grass. The predators and carrion eaters hadn't much gotten to it yet, but the sight of circling turkey buzzards is what had led Chuck to ride over here. The calf had one small hole in its head, right between the bigger holes where its eyes should have been. The buzzards had already eaten the eyes for hors d'oeuvres before Chuck arrived. *Shot with a small caliber, probably just a 22 or 22 magnum*, he thought. Probably shot right from the road, which was just beyond the barbed wire fence, no more than twenty yards from where the two men stood.

The calf hadn't even been gutted properly, the only thing missing was the left hind quarter. Undoubtedly hacked off with great haste in case anyone had heard the shot that killed it. The thought that whoever killed it needed the meat much more than he needed that calf alive, didn't do much to relieve Chuck's sense of anger over having it stolen from him. He had a sense that everything he had known in his sixty-five years of living was being slowly taken away, one thing at a time.

"Guess as hot as it's been, it would only be half-raw if they just left it out in the sun for an hour or two," he replied. "Why do you think they only took the left hind quarter?" He pulled out his comphone and looked at the stock ID screen. Sure enough, it showed calf number 1433 right there in front of him. Of course it did; the BR had been implanting the stock ID chips in the right hind quarter of their stock ever since the ubiquitous ID chips replaced old-fashioned branding.

Chuck looked up at the slowly deteriorating, pot-holed asphalt; what was left of old highway 9. It came over a small rise from the south and disappeared around a bend about a quarter mile away to the north, generally following the route of the Blue River, as it meandered its way downstream to a rendezvous with the Colorado. There was a time, no more than twenty years ago when that highway was fairly busy with constant truck and auto traffic carrying all the freight and tourists of a prosperous nation. Now, there was only Sherriff Larson's electric Jeep sitting in the tall weeds at the side of the road. *Even that Jeep's old by now, probably a twenty-three or twenty-four model. I wonder if anybody still drives new cars*, Chuck thought to himself. He knew that some people somewhere must, but he couldn't remember the last time he'd seen a brand-new personal vehicle.

"Whatever happened to this country, Steve? Or the world for that matter? Remember when we were young, and the world was full of promise? How did we come to this?"

Chuck didn't really expect an answer, and he didn't get one.

"Damn, it's hot," was all Steve had to say.

Damn it's hot, is right, must be the hottest August ever. At least they got enough snow up high last winter that the Blue still has a pretty good stream of water. That's a lot better than last year when it was just a trickle by now.

"You know Steve, we always put our chips in the right hind quarter, not the left. You suppose whoever shot this calf knew that?"

"Nah, probably just a coincidence, most of these city folks passing through don't even know the stock have chips."

That's true, Chuck thought. *But what if it wasn't one of the refugees from the cities?*

"What if it was a local did this? Some of the people right down in Kremmling are hurting some, too."

"They are hurting, but that doesn't make them thieves," the sheriff answered. "Did you ever lose stock before the refugees started coming through?"

"I've always lost a calf or two here and there, a bear, or a lion, but I've got to admit, losing stock to two-legged animals is kind of a new phenomenon."

"That's right, this kind of thing only started when people started emptying out of Texas. That's why I don't think we can blame it on anybody local."

Chuck put his com back in the holster on his left hip and absently reached down to the handle of the gun on his right.

"Guess it really doesn't matter, local or refugee, they better not ever let me catch 'em in the act."

The motion of Chuck putting his hand on his gun wasn't lost on the sheriff.

"Hope you don't plan on doing anything stupid, Chuck. You catch someone, you call me. Let the law deal with this."

The big red quarter horse didn't need any direction from Chuck. He instinctively knew when they were headed for home and set out across the big meadow at a nice brisk walk. Chuck sat the saddle like he was born there. He may not have been born in a saddle, but he had spent a good deal of his life sitting in one.

The big meadow, as it was known, was the largest hay meadow on the Blue River ranch, known simply as the BR by the locals. The big meadow covered roughly two hundred acres of gently sloping grassland, nestled in a big bend of the Blue River where it came down from Frisco Reservoir, flowing north to its confluence with the Colorado River. The grass was short and stubbly now, the hay crop all stacked neatly in the big pole barn which wasn't visible from here; hidden, along with the rest of the ranch buildings, behind the rise at the west end of the big meadow.

Chuck could see the rest of his black angus cattle spread out along the river on the north side of the meadow. *At least they're away from the road*, he thought. *Guess we better move them up to the mesa to keep them safe until we're ready to ship 'em.* There had been forty-five of this year's crop of calves that they'd separated from the main herd to send to Pro Foods. The bulk of the herd was still high in the mountains to the west, grazing on the Forest Service lease that had been part of the BR since before Chuck was born.

Chuck found himself in a reflective mood as he approached the crest of the rise where he could see the BR laid out in the valley near the river. "Whoa Red," a slight pull on the reins brought the big quarter horse to an abrupt stop. He leaned back in the saddle, pushed the brim of the old straw hat up with his free hand and scanned the Blue River and Spider Creek valleys, from the north end of the ranch all the way to the south and the canyon that marked where Spider Creek broke out of the mountains. Spider Creek Canyon was about a mile upstream to the west of the BR headquarters. Hidden from view by the old cottonwood trees lining the river, the remains of Chuck's great-great-grandfather's homestead lay in ruins right up against the rock outcropping, where the rugged rock canyon spilled the Spider out into the wide-open valley to join the Blue. *That's where it all started*, he thought, and then, *that's probably where it'll all end.*

Just a touch of Chuck's heels to Red's side and the horse headed toward the barn at the bottom of the hill.

Instead of continuing on to the barn, with a light touch of the rein on the side of the horse's neck, Chuck turned him toward the large ranch garden where the entire Duran family was busy picking vegetables.

The Duran family had been part of the BR for nearly as long as the BR has existed. Clyde Duran had lived on the BR his entire life. His father, Ben, was Chuck's dad's foreman when Charlie senior had died of a heart attack up on Buck Mountain back in '99. Ben hadn't lived a whole lot longer, also dying of a heart attack in '07. Chuck was only 30 years old when his dad died, and he was suddenly and totally responsible for the operation of the entire BR.

Don't think I could have done it without Ben's help, Chuck thought as he reined up at the gate to the garden. *And now, not without the help of Clyde and his boys.*

The "garden" could have been an entire farmstead for some. It covered the better part of two acres and was entirely enclosed in an eight-foot fence to keep out the deer and elk. Chuck loosely tied Red's reins to the corner post, walked through the open gate and down the rows of tomatoes toward Clyde, who was bent over picking the ripe tomatoes and placing them in an old bushel basket. As he looked over the plentiful crop of tomatoes, Chuck absently thought about how hard it used to be to grow tomatoes this high up. The BR headquarters, at an elevation of nearly 8000 feet hadn't always been the ideal place to grow most vegetables. He had a little inner chuckle as he remembered how his dad, Charlie senior, hadn't believed in climate change.

"Hey Clyde," Chuck said, as he approached the ranch foreman, "you were right about the buzzards, it was another dead calf."

Clyde stretched his back as he turned away from the tomatoes to face Chuck. His long black hair was tied up in the usual single braid that reached to the middle of his back. Other than the thick black hair, his head was bare to the sun. Clyde never wore a hat.

"Yo Chuck," Clyde answered the old rancher. "Just one, then?"

"Yeah, it was just the one. Shot with a small caliber and the left hind quarter gone. Sheriff thinks it was one of those families migrating through from Texas."

"Could be," Clyde mused. "What do you think?"

"I'm not so sure, could be a coincidence that they only took the one hind quarter…or maybe they knew the chip was in the other, and they didn't want it tracking them. How many people around here do you suppose there are that know we put our chips in the left side?"

Clyde glanced over at his two sons who were still busy with the harvest. "Well, besides those two," he said, lifting his chin toward them, "we've had quite a few young folk from round about help us out over the years. S'pose all those that helped with the implants would remember."

"That's kind of what I was thinking. May not be just coincidence that we seem to keep losing just one hind quarter, and it's always the left. Anyway, we better move the rest of the calves up to mesa. Get 'em away from the road. Can you and the boys," Chuck always referred to Clyde's sons, Ralph and Cody, as *the boys,* "take care of that this afternoon? I'll see if I can get the shipment date moved up. Maybe we can get 'em to market before we lose any more."

"You bet." Clyde turned to the boys, "Ralph, Cody, saddle up." Then to his wife, Shellie, "Sorry Shel, we'll be back in a few hours."

Chuck looked over the bounty of the garden, "Looks like I better see if we can get some help with this, too. Probably plenty of folks in Kremmling that'd be glad to help pick veggies for a share. Looks like we have plenty and then some. Hate to see it go to waste."

With Red unsaddled, unbridled, and contentedly chomping on some oats in his stall, Chuck headed to the big house. The big house was a large lodge-style home made of logs. Chuck's father had the big house built when Chuck was just a young boy, back when the oil and natural gas royalties really started coming in. Looking down the lane to the old white clapboard ranch house that the big house replaced, Chuck wondered again about the oddity of him living alone in the big house, while all four of the Duran family lived in the much smaller old house. *It was five,* he thought, *till Anna left*.

He had a sudden memory of seeing James, his grandson, walking with Anna, from the old house down toward the river. It had been a warm summer evening, and the young couple out for an evening stroll had reminded him then, as the memory did now, of similar evening strolls with his late wife, Nancy. The joys of young love. *I should have asked Clyde about Anna*, the thought bothered him. *Wonder how she's doing these days.* A movement in the tall weeds at the edge of his vision caught his eye. The movement of the weeds showed where something was scurrying toward the trees. As he watched, an armadillo appeared out of the weeds in a clear patch of ground. *Guess people ain't the only things leaving Texas,* he thought. *Who would've ever guessed, armadillos in Colorado?*

PART THREE

Chuck doesn't enter the big house through the large front veranda with the massive front double doors. Instead, as always, he walks around the side of the house and in through the mudroom. Seems like the only use he makes of the veranda is to occasionally enjoy a cup of coffee as he watches the sunrise. Of course, drinking real coffee anymore is a rarity, indeed. Mostly, Chuck's morning beverage now is brewed from roasted chicory root.

After grabbing a chunk of roast beef and some homemade cottage cheese, compliments of Shelly Duran, out of the refrigerator, he sits down at the same barstool where he always eats. The bar is all that separates the kitchen from the rest of the huge great room that takes up most of the ground floor of the big house. Chuck always sits on the kitchen side of the bar facing the large comscreen above the fireplace on the other side of the great room.

"Hey Bozo," he says, with a heavy emphasis on the *Bozo*. He still finds simple pleasure in the name he gave to his digital assistant, once the option of selecting your own name replaced the likes of Siri, Alexa, and Google. "News."

The big comscreen flashes to life with a running script scrolling up the screen, as a clear female voice gives the same information, it's as if she's reading the news from a teleprompter. Chuck set up his com this way long ago, finding the videos from the newscast to be too distracting.

-Yesterday's high of 111 degrees has now been confirmed as a new record for Dallas. The previous highest recorded temperature for the month of November was the 106-degree reading on November 7th of last year. -
-On Amerinet, there are rumors of a new flu virus in Europe. Due to ongoing problems with international communications, Colnews can neither confirm nor deny the rumor. There have been no reports of any new virus in this country. The Colorado Department of Public Health has filed a request for information with the CDC in Atlanta. Stay tuned for updates as they become available. -

    Good luck getting anything out of the feds, Chuck thinks. He remembers when the whole world was connected by the internet and you didn't have to rely on the government for information about anything. That was before the Great Mid-East war, of course. Before that dark day when the internet went dead to Americans forever. It had taken well over a year to rebuild the cyberinfrastructure and to bring the Amerinet of today online, even though the government had been secretly developing it for decades. *The feds might control it, and you might not be able to find out about Europe,* Chuck muses, *but at least it's secure from cyberwar and other governments. And what about our own government?* he wonders. *Can't even trust Colorado government, let alone what's left of the Feds. What's left of the Feds seems to be more of a problem than ever,* he thinks. *Sure, the military's been cut down to size, but how many that counted on social security are starving? How many can't even afford that crap they call Allpro?* It bothers Chuck immensely that most of the purebred

Black Angus beef he raises now goes into the production of Allpro. *Not too many of us lucky enough to still eat this,* he thinks, as he takes the last bite of the cold roast beef. *Course there's always those few; politicians, bankers...I'm sure they're still eating steak.* The thought of bankers eating steak reminds him of his daughter and his never-ending quest to understand how she could have ever married a bankster.

"Bozo, music." As usual, the news tends to just be upsetting. The sound of **River Waltz** by the Cowboy Junkies fills the room as Chuck finishes chewing his roast beef. *Plenty of dying rivers to choose from nowadays,* he muses. His thoughts turn to memories of his wife Nancy. Hearing her favorite song always seems to bring out those memories. *God, I miss her! If only she'd gone to the doctor sooner.* It's still a bitter haunting thought, even though ten years have passed since Nancy died of ovarian cancer. *Ten years,* he thinks. *Ten years since she died and Noni hasn't been here since. Hell, it's been years since James has even been here. Guess he must have taken after his worthless father.*

Another thought comes to Chuck, unbidden. A saying from his own youth; *life's a bitch, and then you die.* He tries to shake off the melancholy. *Guess I'm just feeling old,* he thinks, as he finishes the last of his lunch.

Chapter 8

Dateline, May 17, 2035. The eye of Hurricane Ida is expected to pass directly over Philadelphia sometime around midnight tonight...

The throwback dateline was what always brought James back to this particular newsfeed. Something about that dateline made him almost feel like he was living in an earlier time; a better time, when the world didn't seem to be falling apart. James was in his secure apartment on the Colorado College campus in Colorado Springs. The clock in the corner of the screen showed 6:47. *Almost nine in Washington*, he thought. He was getting ready to go to a show at the Fine Arts Center with Julie. Julie was getting ready in the other room.

The storm, which made landfall as a category 5 hurricane earlier this evening has weakened but is still packing 130 mile per hour winds and torrential rains. Damages to the area around the Capitol are expected to be severe, compounded by high tide, which will occur at 11:31 eastern time. According to a statement released earlier today by the White House, the President, members of Congress and the Supreme Court, as well as all other essential government personnel are riding out the storm in an undisclosed secure location in the DC area. In other news, the familiar voice of the newscaster droned on, as James finished knotting his tie, *the army has dispersed a group of rioters, who were attempting to storm the Allpro production plant in Springdale, Arkansas. Army spokesperson, Susan Baker, reports that casualties among the rioters were less than three hundred, with twenty-two army personnel also killed. Warning against further riots, the army cautions that any attempt to subvert food production facilities will be met with lethal force.*

Subvert facilities, what a farce. Knowing the reality; that the starving mobs didn't want to subvert anything, that they only wanted food to eat, just made the melancholy that James had been feeling even more pronounced. *What a world*, he thought. *I'm getting ready to go to a play, while people are starving to death. Fiddling away, while Rome burns.*

All of a sudden, James' thoughts were interrupted by silence. The news had gone silent. He looked at the big screen on the wall. The words, *BREAKING NEWS* were displayed in huge letters across the middle of the screen. Just then, the familiar face of the newscaster came back on the air. She was speaking in the same calm voice as always, but she appeared shaken. *We have just received word from the USGS that a powerful earthquake has been detected in the Atlantic Ocean. Tsunami warnings have been issued for the Atlantic coast from Maine to Florida and the entire Caribbean, as well as the entire western coast of Europe and the northwest coast of Africa. Initial reports indicate a massive earthquake with a magnitude of at least 9 on the Richter Scale. The epicenter of the quake was approximately 1250 miles southeast of Bermuda. We will update this story as news becomes available.*

"Hey Julie," James shouted toward the master bath. "Did you hear that?"

"Hear what?" She stepped out of the bathroom, obviously ready to go. She was wearing a stunning low-cut deep blue gown. Her long blonde curls falling around her shoulders, framing the fine features of her face. Her blue eyes sparkled nearly as much as the diamond necklace that drew attention to the deep cut of the blue gown, and the cleavage exposed at the V of the cut.

As gorgeous as Julie was, James hardly noticed. His thoughts were on the disaster that was unfolding thousands of miles away. "The earthquake! There's been an earthquake in the Atlantic."

Julie looked at James with an expression that seemed to say, so what, what does that have to do with us, before she noticed the truly worried look on his face. She looked up at the newscaster, who now appeared to be actually frightened. She was getting up from behind the news desk, still talking. *We have been told that we have to evacuate the studio here in New York. We transfer you now to our affiliate in Los Angeles.* The camera showed the newscaster being hurriedly ushered away before the feed could be transferred to Los Angeles. *Damn,* James thought, *it's like nature's trying to destroy us. And why not? We've been at war with nature for a long time.*

The screen went blank for a moment, and then a different studio appeared with a man seated behind a desk, much as the woman had been in New York. *Good evening ladies and gentlemen,* the man began. He was dressed in a shirt and jacket that looked like they had been thrown on in a hurry. His lack of makeup seemed unnatural on a newscast. James was struck by the incongruity of the fact that a lack of makeup seemed unnatural, while someone made up to the hilt seemed to be normal. *This nation is in the midst of a natural disaster*, he stammered a little, the teleprompter script obviously out of sync, *a series of catastrophic natural disasters that is unprecedented...*

The man's voice droned on in the background. James sat down in one of the leather chairs opposite the comscreen. "Maybe we better not go," he said absently, as he continued looking at the screen.

Julie wasn't about to give up the play she had been dying to see just because of a weather incident on the other side of the country. "What do you mean, we better not go? To the play? We have to go, it's the final performance."

James turned his attention from the screen to Julie. He knew she was emotionally shallow. That was part of what had attracted her to him. That, her looks, and plain old sexual attraction. At the time, he was really only interested in a sexual relationship, with as little emotion involved as possible. James had met Julie Johnson the day he arrived at Colorado College three years earlier. "Do you really think an off-Broadway play is more important than what's happening on the east coast?"

"Of course not. But we can't do anything about the east coast. Besides, hurricanes hit the east coast all the time. People ought to be used to it by now."

Mentally, James shook his head in disbelief. "Did you not hear them say, tsunami?" he asked incredulously. "Do you know what a tsunami can do?"

"They don't know for sure that a tsunami will hit," Julie pouted.

Flabbergasted, James decided to try another tack. "Diggy, is the play still on at the Fine Arts Center?"

There was a very short delay before the response, "No, the play has been canceled due to events on the east coast."

"Fuck!" It was almost a shout, as Julie stormed back into the bathroom and slammed the door.

Guess I probably won't get any tonight, James thought, as he turned his attention back to the newscast on the big screen. ***We are getting reports of impassable roads, as people try to evacuate coastal areas. With aircraft unable to take off due to Hurricane Ida, if a tsunami does hit, the loss of life and property is expected to be beyond catastrophic.***

Everything's beyond catastrophic these days, he thought. For some reason, his thoughts turned to his arrival at Colorado College. He had arrived in late May, giving himself a week to adjust before classes commenced the first week of June. Convincing his dad that Colorado College would be better for him than Harvard or Yale had been a challenge. *Guess it's a good thing I stayed in Colorado, even if it does mean being in the same state with Dad.* James avoided his father as much as possible. He could hardly stand to talk to him on the com, let alone be in the same room with him. In the end, his father had agreed to Colorado College as a compromise for James promising to never see Anna Duran again.

James had arrived in Colorado Springs riding alone in his Jeep, with no escort or security of any kind. It had been a bit of a shock when he saw the perimeter wall that was nearly completed around the campus. There had been a security fence around Colorado One, but it was nothing like the wall that now surrounded the entire campus of Colorado College. This was a thirty-foot-tall structure made of precast concrete panels topped with razor wire. He remembered having a thought when he first saw that wall, *am I going to college or to prison?* Outside the wall, the City of Colorado Springs had been a total mess. The streets were littered with debris. Most of the old storefronts were either boarded up and vacant or standing empty with broken glass and broken doors. Some of the open doorways he passed had haggard looking people staring out at him. There were a few businesses still open, and they not only had bars on all the windows, they were protected, not by private security people, but by the U.S. military. Some had Air Force troops while others had groups of Army troops standing at the entrance. All were heavily armed. James remembered how strange it had been to see so many military people and not one member of a civilian police unit. Thinking back on it now, he had the thought; *military town to the very end.*

Like the businesses on the way in, the entrance to Colorado College had been guarded by a group of heavily armed army personnel. With a gate across the road and two armored vehicles for good measure, it had reminded James of news clips from his childhood of military checkpoints in places like Afghanistan and Iraq. He hadn't had any trouble getting through the checkpoint, of course. The sergeant, who seemed to be in command, had simply wondered out loud how the hell James had arrived without any security detail. Once inside the checkpoint, it had been like another world. Colorado College was like a thriving small city inside the vast ruins of a once thriving metropolis. He had pulled into a nearly empty parking lot in front of the apartment building he had been assigned to and had no trouble at all finding an empty charge station. Nearly all of the parking spaces had charge stations, but there were only three other vehicles in the entire lot. Wondering, as he fitted the plug to the port on his Jeep, where all of the cars could be; that question was answered by what he saw coming through the barricade behind him. It was a convoy. At first, it seemed like a military convoy, with a military-style armored vehicle in the lead and another in the rear. But the vehicle in the middle was definitely not military. It was a black stretch limo.

James watched as the convoy pulled up in front of the building, stopped, and two people got out of the limo. He recognized the woman who stepped out of the limo first. It was Senator Jill Johnson. Julie Johnson had stepped out of the limo next. It was the first time James saw Julie.

As he remembered how the convoy had left Julie at the school that day, he wondered, *is Senator Johnson in Washington?*

His thoughts were interrupted by silence. He realized that the newscast was silent and looked at the screen. It was blank. "Julie," he spoke to the closed bathroom door. No answer. He walked over to the door and knocked. "Julie, is your mother in Washington?" There was still no answer, but he could hear muffled sobs from the other side of the door. He tried the knob, it wasn't locked. He opened the door slowly to give her time to react if she was going to, and then went in.

Julie was sitting on the toilet in just her panties and bra. The fine blue gown was in a heap in the middle of the bathroom floor. She had her face in her hands and was sobbing. Loudly, he noticed, now that he was not on the other side of the door. "Julie, Julie honey," he tried to console her, kneeling and putting an arm around her shoulders. "It'll be okay. They'll protect your mom." Even as he said it, he wondered who he thought *they* were, and how *they,* no matter who they were, could protect anyone from the terrible wrath of nature.

The rising sun shining brightly through the living room window woke James with a start. His neck was stiff from the awkward position he'd been sleeping in, still fully dressed, slumped in the easy chair in front of the comscreen. A commercial was blaring from the com. The same Allpro commercial that seemed to be on the air more than all other programming combined.

... it's not just good for you, it's good for America.

James stood up and stretched. He was hungry and wondered, as he had before, if there was something psychological about the commercial that brought on hunger. *Just what the starving masses need,* he thought, *something to remind them how hungry they are.* He walked into the bedroom to find Julie stretched across the bed sideways, still dressed in nothing but the pale pink bikini panties she'd been wearing the night before. She'd taken off the bra, which lay near the foot of the bed. She had obviously cried herself to sleep at some point. There was something about the vulnerability of her lying there asleep on her stomach, nearly naked, that made him horny. *Great*, he thought, as he rearranged the unwanted erection that was straining uncomfortably against the confinement of his jeans. *I'm not only hungry, but I'm horny. Nero fiddled while Rome burned, I'm ready to screw as America ends.*

That unbidden thought, *as America ends*, brought him up short. The erection was gone as quickly as it had materialized. He turned quietly, so as to let Julie sleep, left and went back to the living room. He turned the com volume down, as he turned his attention back to the screen. There was a female newscaster on screen now, and James didn't recognize her any more than he had known the man from the night before. Unlike that man from last night, she was made-up and looked professional in every way, right down to the extremely worried look she portrayed as she spoke.

... communication with the Federal Government in Washington has not been restored. We have also been unable to reach our New York affiliate. We do know that a tsunami hit the Atlantic coast of the United States at approximately 1:15 a.m. eastern time, but the extent of the damage is unknown. Tsunami warnings for Europe and all other locations have now been canceled.

Something on the woman's teleprompter caused her to pause and look questioningly off camera to her right. She turned back to face the camera. She was visibly shaken.

We have now acquired new video that we have reason to believe was captured by someone in Ocean City, Delaware. We believe the footage was being transmitted live as it was shot, otherwise, it would have been lost. No other details are available. The video you are about to see is disturbing, to say the least.

The scene on the screen was dark and grainy. At first, it was hard to make out anything but a few specks of light. Slowly, it became clear that it was not only darkness obscuring the scene, but sheets of torrential rain as well. There were gaps in the rain as one sheet of rain would pass, with an open gap before the next sheet of rain obscured the view. The view, when not totally obscured, was one of a mostly darkened city, with some buildings lit by what had to be emergency lighting. There was one building, in particular, that really stood out. It appeared to be seven or eight stories tall and must have had extremely good emergency lighting. It seemed like most of the building's windows were lit up. It was hard to make out any detail, but the building seemed to be a block or two from where the videographer was standing. There didn't seem to be any buildings beyond the one that was all lit up, and then, in a moment devoid of any rain, it became obvious why there were no other buildings beyond that one. A beach could be faintly seen on the other side of the well-lit building, with the darkness of what had to be the ocean just beyond. There was sound with the video. The howling of the wind and the driving rain. Then there was another sound, like a roar in the distance. It reminded James of the roar of a jet engine. The roar quickly grew louder, like a jet was coming down a runway toward the camera, and then it seemed like a wall appeared where the ocean should have been. In a matter of seconds, through a long break in the rain, it became obvious what the wall was.

James watched in morbid fascination as the wall of water, that was a tsunami wave, completely engulfed the lit up building. The wall of water had to have been at least twice the height of the building it devoured, maybe even three times as tall. It was hard to believe his eyes, the sight was so unworldly. *How could something like that be real?* The screen suddenly went black and silent.

James stood staring at the dark screen, his mind having trouble coming to grips with the scale of the disaster that had just hit the east coast. No, not hit the east coast; it was obvious that the tsunami had totally wiped out parts of the east coast. Nothing could survive the wall of water that he had seen with his own eyes. The sea walls and levies that had been built over the previous decade in response to rising sea levels might have protected most places from Hurricane Ida, but nothing could protect anyplace or anyone from a tsunami like the one that hit that building. It was as if the earth itself had struck at the heart of America; retribution for the long war man had waged against nature.

It was then he became aware of Julie standing in the bedroom doorway. Her normally pale complexion had gone totally white, accented by the dark streaks of mascara running down her face, like some kind of ancient war paint. She stood stock still with her arms at her sides. The tears had stopped long ago, and now she seemed to be staring almost blankly at the blank screen. *She's in shock*, he thought, and then; *hell, we're probably all in shock*. At that moment, he felt an overwhelming pity for her. Had she just lost her parents? Washington wasn't on the coast, had it been spared? Where were her parents when the tsunami struck? He walked over and put both arms around her pulling her in tight. She remained unmoving, unresponsive to the hug.

With his back to the screen, James didn't see the newscaster come back on the air, but he heard her say, *I can't*. She seemed to be sobbing, as she spoke. With Julie totally unresponsive to his touch, he let her go and turned back to look at the screen. Just as he did so, three men dressed in military uniforms walked onto the set amid some commotion in the background. In what almost seemed to be a choreographed performance, two of the men grabbed the newscaster by her arms and gently lifted her out of her chair. She didn't resist at all as they escorted her off camera and the third military man took her seat.

My fellow Americans, I am sorry you had to witness the fake news that was just forced upon you. This is an obvious attempt by certain factions in the military to sow doubt and discord among us.

Fake news? Could the whole thing have been faked? Obviously, it could have, but it didn't feel right. Why James wondered, was someone, who he presumed was a general, at the studio to start with. The news studio would have had military protection to be sure, but a general? He looked at the man again. The four stars on each shoulder definitely screamed general, and it seemed like he should recognize the face, but he couldn't quite place the man.

Rest assured that the government of the United States is safe and secure. In order to maintain that security, the country has been placed under martial law, effective immediately. All banks and financial institutions, as well as all food production and distribution facilities, have hereby been placed under direct government control. A nationwide dusk to dawn curfew will take effect immediately. Please remain in your homes after dark.

And what about all of those who have no home, James thought, just as the general let the real bombshell drop.

In order to provide security and to protect the legitimate government of the United States from the forces that assail us, all broadcast systems and all personal communications will be shut down immediately. Please leave all comms in standby mode in order to receive further updates as they are made available. Thank you for your cooperation. God bless America.

The screen went blank and silent. The old Yogi Berra saying came unbidden into James' mind; *it's like deja vu all over again.* "Hey Diggy," he said, knowing there would be no answer. He was remembering that day six years ago when the world went silent. Martial law had gone into effect then, as well; but that time, it had been to restore communications. This time, it seemed to be an effort to squash communications. He turned back to Julie. She was visibly better. She seemed almost relaxed and the color had returned to her face. She wasn't smiling, but the relief on her face was obvious. She had really believed the part about the government being all okay. James didn't. *If the government is all okay,* he thought, *why was a general declaring martial law instead of the President. It didn't make sense. Hell, none of it made any sense.* He wondered, not for the first time, how the world could have changed so much in just the past three years.

He knew it wasn't really just the past three years. His education, here at Colorado College, had truly taught him how much of a bubble he lived in. He had been shielded and protected from reality while attending Colorado One. Sure, he had seen plenty of homeless people, and knew that the world was divided into the haves and the have nots; but he hadn't known at the time just how many have nots there were; and how few there were, like him, that had it all. He had also known nothing of the rebellion against the status quo that had been growing for years. He lost his ignorance, along with whatever innocence he had left, when he took a course titled, THE UNITED STATES – 50 YEARS OF DECLINE. The course was taught by Dr. Mitchell; an aging professor who was nothing, if not a rebel himself. Dr. Mitchell had refused to teach the approved version of history. He had openly encouraged his students to question everything about government, and especially, everything about the elite and the military who controlled that government. It was not an easy task, teaching the elite children of the ultra-upper class to question their right to the status they enjoyed. Dr. Mitchell's course was one of the first classes James had taken, on his arrival at Colorado College. Fresh off the total shattering of his illusions of his father, James had been one of Dr. Mitchell's most avid students.

It had been a strange experience. All of the students who attended Colorado College were part of the elite that Dr. Mitchell questioned, and most who took his course did so just to earn the history credit. Most of the students thought Dr. Mitchell was just an old man, teaching beyond his time. Many wondered how on earth he was still allowed to teach such nonsense at all. They certainly didn't think of their status as anything but a birthright. Those who had been born unfortunate enough to have nothing just needed to get over it. The natural order of things dictated that these few, who had been born to the wealthy elite, were not only entitled to their place in the world; they were required to maintain their elite status, that the natural order should not be broken.

James, on the other hand, had whole-heartedly accepted the premise that there was nothing "natural" about the current "natural order of things". He had enjoyed Dr. Mitchell's lectures so much that he had started meeting with him for one on one conversations, outside the confines of the lecture hall. The meetings and the conversations hadn't ended when the course did. James had continued seeking conversation with Dr. Mitchell whenever he could. It never ceased to amaze James how much Dr. Mitchell knew of things going on behind the scenes. When the "news" had a story about an Allpro shipment being hijacked by domestic terrorists, and how the military would deal with those terrorists; Dr. Mitchell had pointed out the fact that all shipments of Allpro, or any other food, for that matter, were now protected by military convoy. The news story hadn't mentioned any casualties at all. How could that be? Dr. Mitchell – John, as he'd insisted James call him, had not only known the proper question, he had also known the answer. It was through John that James had learned of the growing rebellion in the ranks of the military.

James had always known that the military served the Federal Government, just as the Federal Government served those who allowed the politicians to be in office. What he hadn't thought much about, at least not before he met John, was who makes up the military? Through John, he learned that most rank and file military personnel were there because it was their only means of escaping poverty and hunger. It was an unspoken fact: join the Army, and you'll always have enough to eat. You may have to leave home and loved ones behind, starving; but you, yourself, won't go hungry. "How many of those recruits do you suppose there are," John had asked, "who would like to be able to feed the ones they left back home? How many do you think there are, in this day and age, who are truly loyal to the government; or maybe I should say, to those behind the government."

Julie had gone back into the bathroom and James could hear the shower running. He shook his head. She really does think all is well, he thought. She'll soak in that shower for an hour, while the "normal" people in Colorado Springs are rationed to a few gallons per day at most. He needed to talk to John Mitchell. Everything was definitely not okay. Maybe John would be able to tell him just how not okay things really were. He stepped into the bathroom and yelled loud enough for Julie to hear, "I'm going to see Doctor Mitchell, I'll be back in a little while."

A pleasant "okay," was her only reply, and then he heard her humming a tune. He was shaking his head in disbelief, as he walked out of the bathroom.

Chapter 9

The apartment that James and Julie shared was in the newest and nicest student housing building. They actually had the entire top floor to themselves. There were four apartments on each level. Julie and James had adjoining apartments, and the other two were vacant. Julie still had a lot of things in her apartment, but they mostly lived in James'. The building was only two stories tall, with a parking garage and storage underneath, but it sat on a hill at the far northwest corner of the campus. With the building on high ground, the big picture window in the living room of James' apartment looked out east over most of the campus of Colorado College. As he walked by the window, he could see the sun rising over the plains to the east, then something else caught his eye. There seemed to be some kind of commotion at the front gate.

The front gate, with the back gate always closed and locked, was the only way in or out of campus. It was about a quarter of a mile away from James' apartment. The gate was always guarded by a military detail of some kind with a couple of armored vehicles which always sat with their guns pointed out at the city. Only now, the armored vehicles were moving. As he watched, four soldiers came out of the guard barracks and piled into the armored vehicles which had pulled up to the entrance gate. The gates swung up out of the way and the two vehicles sped through the opening, turned right on the street out front, and disappeared from view behind the wall that surrounded the campus. The gates didn't close.

Trying to make sense of what was happening, he looked over the rest of the campus. About half-way between where he stood and the front gate was the coffee shop where he knew John Mitchell usually spent this time of the morning. That was where James planned on talking to the old professor. The entrance to the coffee shop faced back toward his apartment building. The front gate wasn't visible at all from there. This time of the morning, the coffee shop was probably the busiest place on campus. The normalcy of students and faculty going in and out of the coffee shop was a sharp contrast to the anything but normal events of the past night, and especially to the abnormality of the gates standing wide open, with no one guarding the entrance at all. Suddenly, he saw another military vehicle come from the opposite direction of the ones that had just left. It was another armored vehicle with some kind of machine gun mounted on top; a man sitting behind the gun was sweeping it from side to side, as the vehicle turned the corner and entered the gate. At first, James thought it must be replacements for the soldiers who had just left, but when another identical vehicle came around the corner, followed by another, he knew something wasn't right. The three light armored vehicles were followed by four army trucks and then five buses, which were also painted army green. The convoy of vehicles didn't stop at the entrance but pulled up to a stop right in front of the coffee shop and the campus grocery that was right next door. Two more light armored vehicles brought up the rear, but they did stop at the gates. Instead of taking up positions with their guns aimed out at the city, however, they stopped, blocking the gates, with their guns aimed at the campus itself. As soon as they came to a stop, troops started piling out of the first bus. They were all armed with assault rifles and fanned out quickly. There must have been at least fifty of them. They were outfitted in full battle gear. It looked like an invasion.

It is an invasion! The thought struck James like a physical blow. He watched in horror, as some of the soldiers started rounding up the students and faculty members who had gathered in front of the coffee shop. Other soldiers entered the coffee shop and rounded up those still inside. Other soldiers were fanning out in groups of two or three spreading out across campus. As the soldiers from the first bus were scattering out across campus, more people started pouring out of the second bus. At the same time, the first of the trucks turned and backed up to the front of the campus grocery. The second bus was smaller than the first. Probably no more than thirty people piled out. None were dressed in army fatigues, and none had weapons. At least not any visible weapons. They looked to James like the homeless people or refugees who seemed to be everywhere these days. Some of their clothes looked tattered, and a few weren't even wearing shirts. With the temperature already in the upper eighties, they didn't really need shirts. Unlike the soldiers whose body armor made it impossible to distinguish gender, there were definitely both men and women in the second group. They didn't seem as efficient or orderly as the soldiers, but they did move as a somewhat orderly group toward the truck that had backed up to the grocery store entrance. The truck that had stopped momentarily, proceeded to back right through the large plate glass entrance to the store and then pulled forward. Two of the soldiers, who preceded the civilians, then used the butt of their rifles to smash out any jagged edges of the remaining glass. The civilians, no longer orderly at all, thronged through the broken storefront and disappeared inside. Meanwhile, the soldiers started herding the students and faculty members toward the buses at gunpoint.

James didn't wait to see more. He ran back into the bathroom, where Julie was still in the shower, singing, of all things. "Out!" he yelled. "Get out now!"

"What?" Julie started to say, as he tore open the door and grabbed her. She had obviously finished washing and was just enjoying standing under the running water. *Wasting precious water, as usual*, he thought, as he slammed the water off.

He forced the towel into her hands. "Hurry. Get dressed. We've got to get out of here."

About to protest, the urgency in James' voice cut Julie short. There was a fear in his voice that was contagious. Hurriedly, she wrung some of the water out of her hair and made a few quick swipes with the towel before dashing off to the closet. James, who had headed back out to the living room hollered back at her, "Jeans and a shirt. Comfortable shoes. HURRY!"

As quickly as she could, she got dressed and headed to the living room carrying her running shoes. She found James looking out the front window from a position off to one side. She was shocked to see a gun in his hand.

"Stay away from the window." It was clearly a command, not a request. By now, the soldiers were herding the first group of students and faculty from the coffee shop into the third bus. James thought he could see the pure white-haired head of his old friend and professor, John Mitchell, among the first of those to be forced onto the bus. The back three buses had bars on the windows, obviously some kind of prisoner transport. Just then, one of the students behind Dr. Mitchell must have decided he wouldn't be herded into a prison bus like an animal. He broke free of the group and started to run toward the science building. He hadn't made it more than ten yards when two of the soldiers opened fire; the bullets tearing into his back propelled him forward in a dive to the ground. His legs kicked a couple of times like they were still trying to run, and then he lay still.

Julie, who was sitting on the sofa tying her shoes, herd the gunshots. "James, what is it? What's going on?" she demanded. She was no longer afraid. She was terrified.

James was watching the soldiers, who now seemed to be going building to building, rounding up everyone on campus. He noticed that they seemed to be totally bypassing some buildings and breaking into others, herding the occupants out one building at a time. *How do they know which buildings to break into,* he thought? Then he noticed that each group of soldiers had one person carrying what appeared to be some kind of electronic device with a small antenna, scanning the buildings as they went. Then it dawned on him, the general in the newscast had specifically told everyone to keep their coms on standby. They were tracking people down using the signal from their coms. He stuffed the gun into his pants and grabbed his com. "Where's your com?" he yelled at Julie, louder than he had meant to.

Julie burst into tears again. "I don't know, on the nightstand?" she asked, looking around as if she could see it from her sitting position on the sofa.

James rushed into the bedroom. Sure enough, her com was there. He grabbed it and hurried back out into the living room. Julie had stood up and was standing squarely in front of the window, her mouth agape. As he grabbed her by the arm and pulled her away from the window, he got a glimpse of the front of the grocery. The civilians, who had arrived with the soldiers, were now going in and out of the store carrying its contents out and loading the trucks. They were stealing all the food from the campus grocery. Most were stuffing handfuls of whatever they could find into their mouths as they went. James had to wonder what it would be like to be that hungry.

"Come on," he said, still pulling Julie by the arm. She started following on her own, and he dropped her arm, as he went out the door, looking both ways, up and down the empty corridor. He ran toward the stairwell at the end of the hall, looking back to make sure Julie was running behind him. He burst through the door into the stairwell and took the stairs three at a time. He paused at the first-floor landing just long enough to yell back at Julie to wait here. He charged through the door into the corridor that ran from one end of this floor to the other. The two floors of the building were laid out identically. At the midpoint of the hallway, there was an elevator alcove with a couple of chairs and a table. James, making sure they were both still on and in standby mode, stuffed his and Julie's coms down in between the cushions of one of the chairs. He sprinted back toward the stairwell just as Julie started to come through the door. Not wanting any of the residents of this floor to know he was there, he didn't yell, instead, he waved her back, as he ran toward her.

James looked over his shoulder once to make sure no one had seen him, before silently pushing Julie back into the stairwell and bounding down the stairs to the underground parking and storage area. Julie followed him, silently now, like a lost kitten trying to keep up.

The basement, designed with eight parking stalls seemed strangely empty, with only two vehicles parked there. James had a moment of longing, as he ran right past his Jeep to the other side of the basement. Opposite the parking stalls, there were ten doors lined up across the entire side of the basement. Illuminated by the twenty-four-hour security lighting, the sign on the first door read: Mechanical. The next room was Maintenance, and then there was a storage room for each of the building's eight apartments. James ran straight to the maintenance room and, knowing it would be locked, threw his shoulder into the door trying to force it open. The impact didn't seem to move the door at all, but it definitely hurt like hell. He stood back and tried kicking the door open. That didn't work either. He pulled the gun out of his pants and aimed at the lock, but he didn't pull the trigger. The last thing he needed was for the soldiers to hear a gunshot. *I need a crowbar,* he thought. That's what he wanted to get out of the maintenance room. Looking around he ran down the row of doors to number seven, which was his storeroom. Maybe an axe would work. He had an axe, along with other camping supplies in storage. The storeroom lock was a four-digit code. He punched in the code on the keypad and pushed the door open.

It had been years since James had used any of the camping supplies that he had in the storage room. He had brought all of the equipment with him three years ago when he first arrived at Colorado College. Back then, he had visions of being able to go off into the foothills and mountains to the west on his own. That was before he knew how unsafe it was to venture beyond the confines of the campus. Hurrying, but not wanting to leave something they might need, James rummaged through his things. He grabbed a backpack and looked inside. It was as he'd left it, with most everything needed for a day hike, other than food, still packed up and ready to go. He pulled a jacket and a raincoat out to make more room in the pack. With the temperature hardly ever dropping below sixty anymore, there wasn't much chance of needing warm clothing. On some shelves in the corner of the room, there were some dehydrated food pouches, vacuum sealed mylar bags of jerky, and some similar bags of nuts. Scooping the food into the pack quickly, as well as a six-pack of bottled water, he closed the zipper and slung the pack over his shoulder. The axe was leaning against the end of the shelves. He grabbed it and turned back to the door. *Hope this will work*, he thought.

Julie was standing just outside the door, watching. Her pale complexion was white with fear; her hair, still damp, hung down to her shoulders in long curly strings. She didn't say a word, as James led her, running again, toward the door to the outside stairs that led up to ground level from the basement. The outside entrance to the parking garage came out on the back side of the apartment building, opposite the side that faced the main entrance to the college. James' only hope, as they climbed those stairs, was that none of the soldiers had yet worked their way around behind the building. He poked his head up above the stairwell enough to scan the surroundings.

The security wall, prison wall, as John used to call it, was no more than fifty yards to the west of the apartment. The grounds of the campus were xeriscaped, with red gravel from the stairs to a concrete path that James knew ran around the entire perimeter. There was a space between the path and the wall that was planted with drought hardy shrubs and trees. The width of the area between the path and the wall varied, as the wall was straight, while the path meandered in curves. James had walked that perimeter path with John Mitchell many times. The old professor had loved walking the path, discussing history and current events.

There was no one in sight, but the sounds of the chaos from the other side of campus echoed off the wall. There was a lot of yelling and then some more gunshots. James spoke quietly, just above a whisper. "We have to get over to the wall. There's a space between the wall and the path where we can hide in the brush, ready?"

Julie nodded, her eyes wide with fear. James, carrying the axe in his left hand, grabbed her hand with his right and ran straight toward the wall. Without looking back, he practically dragged her across the path and crashed through the undergrowth. Dragging Julie behind him, he crawled into a small space between the wall and some Mormon tea plants. They had to stay crouched down, the plantings here were only about four feet tall. Julie was whimpering. He wasn't sure, as he looked at her, if it was because of the bloody scratches on her arms, or just the situation, in general. Seeing the scratches from the brush, he could feel how scratched up his own arms were. Ignoring the scrapes and scratches, he peered out through openings in the brush. *So far, so good,* he thought. He still couldn't see anyone. The buildings blocked his view of what was happening on the other side, which meant they blocked anyone from seeing this way, as well.

Taking his bearings, he wasn't sure which way to go. He hesitated trying to remember where it was. He remembered the day John had shown it to him. They had been on one of their usual walks around campus. John had seemed unusually agitated that day. James remembered him saying that it had to end, that a revolution was past due in the United States. "We can't hide behind walls forever," he'd said, gesturing at the security wall, "while the rest of the world falls apart." It had been a frequent topic of discussion. John knew who James' father was, and how he manipulated the strings of power. He seemed to have a true sense that James did not, of just how bad things were on the other side of society. Other than occasionally seeing homeless people and refugees on the streets, James had been sheltered from the economic and climatologic disasters of the previous two decades. His only experiences with "normal" people had been during his trips to the Blue River Ranch. He hadn't argued with John that day, but he hadn't really believed a revolution was possible either. He believed it now.

It had to be north, he thought. *It was closer to the northwest corner of the wall.* "Come on," he said to Julie, who was still whimpering softly, "we have to get out."

Walking in a low crouch where the brush was tall enough to shield them, and crawling on hands and knees where it wasn't, they made their way north along the wall. Crawling almost on his belly through a particularly tight spot between the wall and some kind of thorny brush, James came out into a cleared area that was larger than any they had yet seen. Next to the wall, at the edge of the clearing, there was a metal lid, or door, on some kind of underground vault. *There it is.* He had a strange tingle of elation, as he stood up. This clearing was well shielded from view. As he walked across the clearing, memories of John showing him this vault came back, as clearly as if it had been just yesterday.

It had been a hot day the previous summer when John had stopped walking along the path to look around. No one else was out, it was too hot. John had made sure they were alone before saying to James, "Follow me, I need to show you something." Amused, but curious, James had followed as John carefully worked his way through the brush to this opening.

"When the time comes," he'd said, pointing at the underground vault, "this is the way out."

"When the time comes?" James had asked.

John Mitchell had gestured at the wall by pointing with his chin. "When that really is a prison wall," he'd said.

Now, looking up at the wall, James remembered how skeptical he'd been at the time. He remembered thinking that maybe his good friend, Dr. Mitchell, had finally lost it. *Guess it wasn't John that went off the deep end,* he thought, *it was the rest of world out there.*

The door to the vault had a hasp type lock with an old-fashioned padlock securing it. James tried using the blade of the axe to pry the lock open. It wasn't working. That's why he had wanted to get into the maintenance room; he'd hoped to find a crowbar. The sound of more gunfire in the distance gave him hope that no one would hear as, giving up on prying the lock off, he swung the axe like a sledgehammer, striking the lock with such force that it not only sprung open, it shot across the clearing, missing Julie by just a few inches.

"I can't go in there," he heard Julie say, as he swung open the lid. "I'm claustrophobic."

Oh great, he thought. *Now's a fine time to find out.* "We don't have a choice, Julie. There's no other way." He rummaged in his pack until he found the headlamp stashed in the bottom. The light from the opened hatchway revealed the top of the built-in ladder that descended into the vault. Relieved to see the headlamp batteries still had juice, James shined the light down to reveal the inside of the vault. The concrete walls extended to the floor, which appeared to be a good ten or twelve feet down from the surface. The built-in ladder went straight down the south wall. There were tunnel openings in the east and west walls at the bottom of the vault, with multiple pipes and conduits running from one tunnel opening to the other. The pipes and conduits had valves and control boxes of some kind mounted to the floor and the north wall of the vault. It appeared that all of the utilities were mounted on the north side of the tunnel as well; leaving a space to walk through the tunnel along the south wall.

Julie had backed a couple of feet away from the open vault. She was obviously terrified. Just as James was hoping she was more terrified of the soldiers on campus than she was of the confined space of the vault, loud shouts came from the direction of their building. Someone yelled, "stop or I'll shoot!" They could hear the sound of someone running along the path on the other side of the brush. Then they heard the blast of two gunshots, and something, presumably the runner, crashed into the brush, no more than fifty feet away. James had the sudden fear that he may not have been the only person, other than John Mitchell, who knew about the tunnel. If others knew, they might accidentally lead the soldiers to them.

He jumped up and grabbed Julie, who was actually shaking, and started pulling her to the vault. "Now! We have to go now!" he hissed, in a loud whisper. Julie whimpered, softly at least, as she allowed him to pull her to the opening. Carefully controlling the volume of his whisper, James implored her, "close your eyes, go down by feel. Pretend it's just a ladder out in the open." He helped guide her to the top rung, wishing she would go faster, as she closed her eyes and felt her way down the ladder, shaking and whimpering as she went. As quickly as he could, once Julie had cleared the top two rungs of the ladder, he started down behind her, pulling the hatch lid closed above them. James' foot hit something that felt different from the ladder rungs just as he heard Julie squeal. He'd stepped on her hand. When Julie reached the bottom, she hadn't let go of the ladder but was standing on the floor, holding on and still shaking. Turning his head down, James could see from the light of his headlamp that Julie still had her eyes closed, and seemed to be paralyzed with fear. She had pulled the hand he'd stepped on out of the way, but still held tightly to the ladder with other.

"Julie," he said, as softly and calmly as he could, "you have to let go and back away from the ladder." He could see her shaking her head sideways, still trembling. The ladder wasn't really a ladder, as such, but consisted of individual rungs that were U shaped with the legs of each rung embedded in the concrete wall. The rungs protruded from the wall some four or five inches, and James decided that he was going to have to squeeze past Julie by using the side legs of the rung for a ladder. The fear of being caught, trapped half-way down into the vault was overpowering. Squeezing past Julie with the backpack on wasn't easy, but he finally reached the bottom by literally shoving her sideways. She refused to release her grip on the ladder, and she was still trembling all over, tears were being squeezed out of her tightly closed eyelids. James placed one hand over the hand that held the ladder and wrapped his other arm around her, pulling her in close, he whispered in her ear, "Julie honey, you have to open your eyes. You can do this. Please. You have to do this for me. I need you." The trembling subsided some as he held her close, and after a few seconds that seemed like hours, she opened her eyes, only to be blinded by the light from James' headlamp.

"I can't see," she said, much too loudly to suit James. "Your light's blinding me."

James almost laughed, in spite of himself, as he turned his head, so the light was out of her eyes. The light now revealed the tunnel leading off to the west; straight as an arrow, fading into the blackness beyond the reach of the headlamp's beam. As he gently pulled her clenched hand off of the ladder and pulled her toward the opening he had to wonder where they were going. Not just the location of where they would physically end up, but the where, or what, of a totally unknown future.

Chapter 10

It seemed the tunnel had no end. It was only about six feet from the concrete floor to the ceiling, not quite tall enough for James' six-two frame, which meant he had to walk in an uncomfortable bent over position. They were slogging through water puddled on the floor in most places, and several times they came to places where there were tees in the largest pipe, which had to be a water line. Smaller pipes would tee off from the mainline and cross the tunnel opening, only to disappear into the concrete wall. There were always valves at these pipe junctions which took up much of the room in the tunnel, making it difficult to squeeze past.

James pulled his right leg sideways off of the pipe he was straddling. This was a particularly tight spot, which he'd had to squeeze through sideways; his back rubbing the tunnel wall, while he was almost bear-hugging the six-inch pipe that protruded from the ceiling to just above the nut on top of the valve. The wall of the tunnel, as well as the pipes and conduits, were wet and slimy. Julie had to be cold. *Hell, I'm cold,* he thought, as he tried to straighten and turn to shine the light for Julie. Straightening too much, he bumped his head, once again, on the concrete ceiling.

"Ouch! Damn it!" he exclaimed, too loudly in the enclosed space. Julie jumped slightly at his outburst shattering the silence. Without saying a word; she hadn't said a word since they entered the tunnel, she started climbing over the obstruction. "Be careful," James whispered, "this is a tight one." He heard the sound of tearing cloth as she slid off the pipe to stand next to him. Her jeans had caught on one of the valve bolts and she'd ripped a hole in the thigh of her muddy wet jeans. A small whimper was the only sound to escape her lips, even though he could see her shivering in the lamplight. James turned back around, in his crouched position, and continued slogging through the tunnel. His back and neck were starting to ache from walking crouched over. *Wish I was only five-six like Julie*, he thought.

Finally, they came to a vault opening in the tunnel similar to the one they'd used to enter. James, telling Julie to wait at the bottom, climbed the ladder and tried to open the hatch. No luck. He braced his feet firmly on the ladder and pushed as hard as he could with his back and shoulders, but the hatch door wouldn't budge. Then, he got lower on the ladder so he could push up with one hand while pounding upwards on the aluminum door with the other. That didn't work either. Not only did it not work, but the pounding definitely made too much noise to suit him. *God damn it! Why didn't I bring the axe? Now what?* he thought as he climbed back down the ladder.

Julie, standing right where he'd left her, still shivering, finally spoke. "We're trapped, aren't we? My God! What are we going to do?"

Hearing her voice, edging on hysteria, James knew he had to soothe her, even if he, himself, wasn't sure what they should do. "We're not trapped, there'll be another opening farther on. One that won't be locked from the outside," he added, hurriedly. He hoped he was right, even as he considered going back for the axe. Deciding against that idea, he stooped down again and headed on through the next section of the tunnel.

After what seemed like another eternity of walking in such a stooped over posture that he didn't know if he'd ever be able to stand straight again, James could see a wall in front of him. He thought maybe they were approaching a bend or a junction in the tunnel when the ceiling of the tunnel suddenly opened up above James' head. It felt so good to stand up straight again, that it took him a couple of moments to notice that this opening wasn't like the other two vaults. It was a round opening, about five feet across. Like the other vaults, there were steps embedded in the wall leading up into the opening. Shining the light up toward the top, he could see that the circular opening narrowed as it rose. It was the inside of an offset cone, with the top of the cone only about two feet in diameter. James had never been inside a manhole, but he recognized one when he saw it. At the top, he could see the rusted bottom of a cast iron cover. At least it wasn't another aluminum hatch opening. He climbed up the ladder and was elated to find that, although it was heavy, the cast iron cover could be pushed upwards. As the cover cleared the rim, the daylight above was blinding, even though he had only lifted it up an inch or so. He lowered the lid back into place. He had no idea where they were. He knew they had to be some distance west of Interstate 25; how far, he couldn't guess. Not only did he not know how far west, but he knew nothing about Colorado Springs over on the west side of the interstate. He was trying to decide if he should go back down and wait for nightfall when Julie's scream echoed loudly around him.

She had obviously seen the daylight shining through the slightly opened lid; for her, the proverbial light at the end of the tunnel. Having the light snuffed out again was simply too much. "Open the goddamned lid!" she shrieked. "I can't stand it." She was already reaching for the step to start up behind him.

His mind made up for him, James shoved the lid up above his head and slid it off to the side. The dazzling blue sky above seemed like heaven. He took another step up, poking his head up out of the hole. He saw nothing. At least not any buildings or sign of people, just an open field of dirt. There were some stubbly grasses here and there, but the drought had decimated what appeared to have been some kind of park or green space.

Once they were up out of the tunnel, the open space didn't provide any cover at all, but there didn't seem to be any need to hide. They were in a low spot with mostly gently rolling red dirt hills surrounding them. Directly west of where they stood, there was a much taller hill with a huge water tank on top. *That's where the water pipe must go*, James thought, looking up at the graffiti-covered tank. He looked at Julie and had to laugh.

"What's so funny?" she asked, clearly offended.

James got his laughter under control, but he was still unable to get over the absurdity of the situation. "You should see yourself," he answered. "You look like a refugee."

Julie did, indeed, look a lot like so many of the refugees and homeless people that seemed to be roaming the streets everywhere; though she was probably dirtier than most. Her blonde hair was all tangled and stringy with streaks of the grime from the tunnel. Her wet clothes, besides having tears from crawling through the tight spots in the tunnel, were filthy. There had been nothing clean or dry in the tunnel they had just escaped from.

"You don't look so hot, yourself," she told him. "What are we doing?" She started shaking again and James knew it wasn't from being cold. She started laughing and crying at the same time. It was hard not to laugh at the site of James covered with grime from head to toe, but she was about to the point of hysteria. "What's happening?" she sobbed. Then, remembering what she'd seen from their apartment; "why were they shooting? They were shooting students! Who are they?" the words came out between sobs.

All James could do was shake his head and mumble, "I don't know." He remembered Dr. Mitchell saying, "when the revolution comes," and he really did know. He didn't want to know, but the truth was inescapable. *What now?* he thought. *What happened to John and all the others that the soldiers had rounded up and loaded into the buses? What was happening elsewhere?* He thought of his family, mostly his mother. Surely, whatever this revolution was, it hadn't affected the Mendez family. His father had never relied on the police and the military; he had his own private army for security. It dawned on him suddenly, *that's the answer. We have to get home to Castle Pines. We'll be safe there.* "Come on," he said, with the same authority he'd used to get Julie through the tunnel. "We can't stay here."

Not knowing exactly where they were, and not knowing anything about the streets on this side of town, James just headed north. As soon as they climbed out of the hollow onto the first rise, city and streets came into full view. He could see what appeared to be a major east-west street about a quarter of a mile to the north. The street seemed to mark the northern edge of the open space they were in. On the other side of the street, there was no more open space, just the urban sprawl of old subdivisions. To the east, I-25 was visible in places and hidden in others. James knew the college was just on the other side of the interstate, due east of where they now stood. He couldn't see any people or any vehicles at all on the streets that were visible from this vantage point, so he decided to just continue heading north. It would probably be easier to just walk along I-25 instead of going across country, but his gut instinct told him that would be a bad idea. If they could walk about twenty miles a day, they should be able to get to Castle Pines in about three days, without using I-25.

Just as they got close to the major east-west street, James heard and then saw, some vehicles coming out from under the I-70 overpass, heading directly toward them. They were army green. It looked like some kind of convoy. His first instinct was to hide, but other than a few scraggly dead juniper trees, which wouldn't hide anything, there was no place at all to hide. Fighting a desire to run, he told Julie to sit down next to one of the dead junipers. He sat beside her, trying to look like a couple of refugees or homeless people.

He had a strange thought; *here we are trying to look homeless. Hell, we might be homeless, for all I know*.

The military convoy didn't even slow down. There were four vehicles in the convoy, two armored vehicles and two trucks, like the ones at the college. They had to have seen James and Julie sitting by the side of the road, but they sped on past heading somewhere to the west. James couldn't help but notice that all four of the vehicles were of the autonomous variety. Either Amerinet and all communications had been restored, or the military had only shut down all civilian communications systems. *Probably the latter,* he thought, as he stood up and pulled Julie to her feet.

There were no other vehicles in sight, nor people for that matter, so James decided this would be as good a place as any to get back over on the east side of the interstate. From his memory of the terrain, it seemed that the trek north would be easier if they were a few miles to the east. As soon as they came out from under the I-25 overpass, James knew where they were. The perimeter fence that surrounded Colorado College stretched out to the east, on the south side of the street. They were just about a hundred yards due north of where they'd entered the tunnel a few hours ago. He had a strong desire to follow the wall to the east and then south to the entrance to the college. *What happened to all of those who had been rounded up? What was the situation inside the wall now? Was there anything he could do to help anyone?* With a nod to the old thought that discretion is the better part of valor, he turned north instead of following the wall and headed up the frontage road that ran parallel to I-25.

They'd walked several blocks north passing abandoned, gutted looking strip malls, and one large forlornly empty shopping mall, when they first saw other people. They were approaching what appeared to be another mall or shopping center of some kind, but this one was anything but empty. It was a hub of activity. It wasn't a mall, James noticed, there was a large King Soopers sign above a line of people; actually, two lines of people. *A functioning grocery store?* The thought was as fleeting as it was hopeful. James knew this was anything but normal, as the razor-wire fencing surrounding the large, mostly empty, parking lot came into view.

They were half a block south of the intersection of the frontage road and what appeared to be another major east-west street. The old King Soopers store and parking lot took up most of the next block on the east side of the frontage road. People were coming and going from the old store from every direction but south. James and Julie were the only ones approaching from the south. That's what James thought at first, anyway. Then he noticed, as they got closer to the intersection, that people were walking down the I-25 off-ramp. Looking up at the overpass, he could see a couple of groups of people walking north on the interstate. Everyone, except those crossing the overpass, seemed to be coming to or leaving from the entrance to the old grocery store. There was a good-sized crowd gathered there. Some had backpacks, some were pulling old toy wagons, and some were pushing old shopping carts. Some had nothing but the clothes on their backs. As they got closer, James could see that people leaving the old store were carrying or hauling the old familiar cans of Allpro. Most also had various sizes and shapes of water containers. That seemed to be it, nothing but Allpro and water.

James led Julie diagonally across the intersection to skirt around those who were crowded in front of the entrance to the parking lot. There were at least twenty or thirty fully armed soldiers guarding the only two apparent openings through the razor wire fencing. The openings were only wide enough for people to get through single-file. One was obviously an entrance and the other an exit. A large hand-painted sign between and above the two openings proclaimed in large letters, *EMERGENCY RATION CENTER #108. LOCAL CITIZENS ONLY*! Below that, in somewhat smaller lettering, it advised everyone to have their IDs out and available for the guards.

One of the small groups of people that had come down from the interstate were on the same side of the street as James and Julie. There were four of them, two men and two women; couples James presumed. They were ahead of James and Julie and had stopped directly across the street from the entrance to the ration center. The two men each had a backpack, but not the women. Their clothes seemed tattered and dirty. *They look like they've hiked a long way*, James thought, as they drew near enough to hear some of what the four were saying to each other.

"We need water," he heard one of the women say. "We won't get it here," one of the men answered. "I'm so hungry," the other woman complained.

The group grew quiet when they noticed James and Julie approaching. At the same time as the group

~ 153 ~

noticed them, James noticed that three armed soldiers were coming across the street toward the group. The soldiers got to the middle of the street, the one in front motioned at all of them with his rifle, while the other two flanked him with their guns raised. "Move on," the lead soldier yelled. "refugees aren't allowed here."

"Please," the woman who'd complained of hunger begged. "We're starving."

Seeing them raise their weapons, James was afraid the soldiers would think they were all together and start shooting. "Come on," he said to the entire group, including Julie. "There's nothing for us here." He led Julie right past the other four people and noticed them fall in behind as he passed. *Better than getting shot,* he thought.

They walked along in silence to the end of the block. James looked back to make sure they weren't being followed by the soldiers. The three soldiers had made their way back to the crowd, but now James noticed that there were groups of soldiers everywhere around the perimeter of the emergency ration center. He wondered how many had been killed simply for being hungry or thirsty. He stopped at the corner of the intersection, deciding where to go. His mind made up, he turned to face the group. "I can get you something to eat and some water, but not here; follow me." He turned, and without looking back, continued walking north.

They'd walked due north about a mile before James decided they were far enough from the soldiers to stop. There was a bridge here where the street they were on crossed a mostly dried up creek bed. There were live cottonwood trees lining the creek, which told James that the creek hadn't dried up completely. James was mighty thirsty himself, by then. It was the middle the day and the temperature had to be approaching a hundred degrees.

"Where are you from?" he asked, as he turned to face the group. He noticed that everyone, including Julie, had a look of quiet desperation on their faces. They'd simply followed someone, anyone, who was willing to lead. "I'm James, and this is Julie," he added when no one said anything.

The woman who had begged the soldiers for food was the first to come out of her stupor. "We used to be from Austin," she said quietly. It was then that James noticed how truly emaciated the four people were. They were rail thin, their clothes hanging loosely from their bodies. Their eyes seemed to be kind of shrunken into their sockets, and their lips were all cracked and dry. *They're like walking skeletons,* he thought.

"Can you really get us some water?" It was the man who seemed to be the group's de facto leader. "I'm Ken." His voice was little more than a whisper. He was so dehydrated that he could hardly speak, James realized.

The interstate had veered off to the west away from the road they were on, and they'd crossed over a hill that now shielded them from the activity back to the south. The road ahead went over another hill, shielding them from the north. James looked around carefully, making sure they were alone, before taking off his pack. He reached down into the bottom of the pack and pulled out the six-pack of bottled water that he'd grabbed from his storage room back at the apartment. "This is all I have," he said as he handed a bottle to each of the group. He twisted the top off of his and only took a sip of the water. Each of the four strangers did the same. They very carefully unscrewed the plastic caps and drank a bit of the water slowly, cautiously; allowing it to bath their parched mouths with precious moisture before they swallowed.

Julie, unlike everyone else, was gulping her water down in big swallows. James reached out and pulled the water bottle down away from her mouth. "Julie, there isn't anymore." He said it quietly, but firmly. "We have to make this last."

For just a moment, the defiant look of over-privilege flashed in Julie's eyes, then the predicament they were in came back to her. "What are we doing, James? Where are we going?" The questions were a plea. It was almost as if she expected him to tell her that all was well, and he'd lead her back to the safe life of ease and plenty that she'd always known. Deep down, that is what James wanted as well. We just have to get home, he thought. Dad will have everything under control, once we get to Castle Pines. He kept trying to think positive thoughts about how his father had a private army and didn't rely on the U.S. military for security; how everything would be just fine, once they got back to where that private army could protect them. *Stay positive,* he thought, *just stay positive.* But try as he might, he couldn't dispel the doubts and dark fears lurking just below the surface.

James looked around some more, deciding they should first get out of the sun. He led the group down around the side of the bridge abutment, into the dry creek bed under the bridge. "Let's just wait out the heat of the day right here," he said, as he sat down on the concrete footing of the bridge that made a perfect bench. As the others sat down as well, he fished in his pack and tossed one of the large bags of trail-mix to Ken. "Not much," he said, "but better than nothing. Hope it isn't too stale."

The gratitude in Ken's eyes was heartbreaking, as he very carefully opened the bag, and doled out a few morsels to each of his companions.

The dire situation that they found themselves in must have finally hit home for Julie. She was seated next to James, on the side opposite their four companions. She leaned over and whispered in his ear. "You can't give them our food. What are we going to eat? I'm hungry too, you know."

For a moment, Julie's selfishness angered James, but then he simply felt sorry for her. Like himself, she had never wanted for anything. Everything in her life had always been all about her. She was a lot like his father, he realized; pretty much devoid of empathy. Is that what had attracted him to Julie? Did he somehow love his father, in spite of Robert's lack of empathy? By extension, did he love Julie, precisely because of that same lack of empathy? He thought of his love for Anna. So much different. *Other than mother, perhaps, Anna is probably the kindest person I know.* The thought filled him with regrets. *And what about me, he thought? How could I have been so cruel?*

His thoughts were interrupted by Ken. "We need to get moving," he said, as much to himself as anyone it seemed. After handing out just a few handfuls of the trail-mix, he had very carefully resealed the bag and tucked it into his backpack. None of the others had complained.

"Wouldn't it be better to travel at night?" James asked. "Or at least not during the worst of the heat?"

Rather than answer his question immediately, Ken just looked at James and Julie before speaking. "What are you two doing out here? It's pretty obvious you haven't been on the road."

The question set James back a bit. It must have been pretty obvious that they couldn't have been on the road for long alright, but how much did he want to share? Not only how much did he want to share, but what did he really know? It seemed that some kind of revolution or military coup had taken place, but he really didn't know much of anything for a certainty.

James decided he would be as truthful as he could. These people didn't seem to be any kind of a threat. "You're right, we haven't been on the road. Near as I can tell, we've just escaped being captured by some kind of renegade army unit; or worse. Maybe the entire U.S. military is renegade, or maybe it's like a coup. I just don't know. I..." the sentence trailed off into thoughtful silence.

"So, you two are government of some kind?" the question, which sounded a lot more like an accusation than a question, came from one of the women, who had yet to introduce herself.

Julie started to respond, "We aren't government, but..."

James cut her off, thinking it might be better not to tell them that Julie's mother was a U.S. Senator. "We were at school. They just came and started rounding up everyone at our school."

Julie must have caught the idea from James that it might be better to keep her mother out of this. "They shot some of the students," she said; "Why would they do that? Why would soldiers shoot students like that?" She seemed to be asking James, as much as the rest of the group.

Julie and James now had all four of the stranger's complete attention, and James wasn't so sure that was a good thing. He was getting some of the same vibes of disdain for the privileged that he remembered feeling while talking to that salesman on the train so very long ago. The four had to know that James and Julie were from the privileged class if they were college students in this day and age. They didn't have to know just how privileged, though.

After a few seconds of silent scrutiny, there seemed to be a softening of attitude among the four. "I'm Darrell." The man who hadn't spoken up until now stuck his hand out and James shook it. "The whole world must really be going to hell if they're shooting college students. Thought it was only us." James wasn't sure who the 'us' referred to. Darrell seemed to be referring to more than just the four of them.

The two women then introduced themselves; Chris and Sarah were their names. Sarah had a coughing fit before she was able to get out her introduction, and James noticed that none of the four seemed to be totally well. How could they be? Up until he shook Sarah's hand, he had attributed their apparent lack of good health to the ordeals of walking so far and an obvious lack of food and water. Sarah's hand was actually hot. He realized that she was not only hungry and thirsty, but she was also ill; unless dehydration could cause one to have a fever.

"Are you ill?" he asked. Not that anything could be done about it if she was, it just seemed like the right thing to say.

"God, I hope not." She actually managed a weak smile. "I sure don't want to end up like some of the others we've come across."

"Have you run into people who were sick?" James asked. He remembered hearing something on the com a month or so ago about some kind of rare spring flu virus or something that was going around.

Sarah looked down at the ground and it was Ken that answered. "Not sick, dead. And not just one or two…" he kind of trailed off and seemed to look back in time. "Too many. Way too many."

James decided he should change the subject. "Why did you leave Austin? On foot, of all things?" He directed the question at Ken and could see by the look on his face just how incredulous the question seemed.

"You really have been in a cocoon, haven't you? Do you know anything about the world out here?" Ken gestured just enough to show that 'out here' encompassed pretty much everything.

James could sense some of the earlier contempt returning to Ken's voice. He started to answer with, "Guess our coms," as he instinctively reached to his side, where his com should have been. It was then that he noticed no one had a com. He knew what had happened to his and Julies, but none of the four strangers had one, either. "Guess our coms," he went on, "haven't kept us very well informed."

"Coms!" It was an outburst from Darrell. "Spreading nothing but fucking propaganda for years. You think you fucking rich people hiding behind your walls learn anything about what's going on by listening to all that crap? You think the government or anybody else really gives a shit when most of Miami's underwater? Or Austin bakes so dry that it's impossible to ship enough water to keep people from dying of thirst? Do you think anybody in the government cares one bit about all of the people who are dying? The government in Washington doesn't care about anybody but people like you! Rich kids, protected at college, while the rest of us die of starvation!"

Darrell had come to his feet during his rant and, for a moment, James thought he might have a fight on his hands. But Darrell sat back down after the outburst and bent over with his head in his hands, his elbows propped on his knees. Julie also had her face in her hands, and she was sobbing again. The other three just sat there looking angrily at James. He didn't know what to say. He stood up slowly, and grabbing Julie by her arm, pulled her to her feet. "Come on," he said softly, turning to leave. He spoke louder over his shoulder to the other four, "guess you probably haven't heard about the tsunami that hit Washington."

"Well, I guess chickens do come home to roost," he heard Ken answer. Then the tone in Ken's voice softened. "James, thanks for the food and water. I wouldn't travel at night if I were you. Best to hide out where they can't see you with night vision goggles."

James could hear Sarah having another coughing fit as he helped Julie scramble back up the embankment to the road. He decided to head back to I-25. Maybe it was the best way to go north. That's the route most were walking; maybe there was some kind of safety in numbers. He and Julie just had to get better at blending in.

Chapter 11

They couldn't have traveled more than seven or eight miles before they came upon the first body lying off the side of the interstate. They smelled it sweltering in the heat before they actually saw it. The body was just over the edge of the embankment, sprawled face first with its head down the hill and bare feet sticking up above the edge of the road. James couldn't tell if it was a man or a woman. Someone had obviously stolen the shoes, and the rotting bare feet had already been pecked apart. Some ravens and a couple of magpies flew up away from the body at James' and Julie's approach. The birds didn't go far, settling down a few yards away to wait for the intruders to leave them to their feast.

It was already getting to be late in the afternoon, and the heat seemed unbearable. They'd been walking along the edge of the interstate; working their way around the few stalled vehicles that they came across. James had been surprised by how few stalled vehicles there actually were. He could remember how many vehicles had stalled and plugged the streets and highways when all autonomous vehicles had died the first time the net and GPS went down. It had also seemed strange that the stalled vehicles all seemed to be personal transportation, not the autonomous semi-truck freight haulers that you'd expect to see on I-25. They hadn't been on I-25 for long when that mystery was solved by the first of many military convoys that were the only vehicles still plying the interstate.

They had been walking along the outside edge of the northbound lanes of the road and heard the convoy approaching from behind before they ever saw it. James' first instinct had been to try to hide from the approaching vehicles, but not only was there no place to hide, there was another group of people a quarter mile or so ahead of them, also trudging northward, who didn't seem to be paying any mind at all to the oncoming convoy. So, James and Julie just got further off to the edge of the road and watched the convoy as it passed them by. The convoy had been led by some kind of light armored non-autonomous vehicle, which was followed by some sort of military vehicle that James had never seen before. It looked like some kind of transport truck that, instead of a normal truck bed, had a large dish antenna looking device mounted on the frame. The antenna was pointed back toward the convoy. James noticed that like the armored vehicle in the lead, the antenna truck was also not autonomous. They both had soldiers manually driving them down the middle of the highway. Directly behind them, however, was a string of five autonomous semi-trucks, two freight vans, and three water tankers, followed by two autonomous armored vehicles bringing up the rear. It was obvious to James that the military, or someone, had shut down the GPS and communications systems that allowed autonomous vehicles to function; and then had the means to get autonomous vehicles to use signals from mobile antennas to lead those vehicles wherever they wanted them to go. *But why?* A real coup or revolution was the only possible answer he could think of. As disturbing as that answer was, it did at least answer the question of what had happened to all of the trucks. What they planned to do with all of the freight, mostly food and water, that they were rounding up was another question.

With no more convoys approaching, James and Julie skirted past the dead body by walking down the middle of the traffic lanes. They were approaching another exit ramp with a road crossing the interstate on an overpass about a quarter of a mile ahead. The sign above the interstate said *EXIT 153 Interquest Parkway.* James wished he could remember more about the Colorado Springs area than he did, but being basically holed up at Colorado College for the past three years hadn't been very conducive to learning what was outside its walls. One thing he did know; they weren't making very good time. The group of people who had been a short way ahead of them when they first started walking along I-25 had left them in the dust. They were now completely out of sight on the other side of the overpass. James was walking a few yards ahead of Julie, wishing she would walk faster, when he heard the sound of her plastic water bottle hitting the pavement behind him.

He stopped and turned to see Julie standing there with her empty water bottle slowly rolling toward the edge of the highway. "Damn it, Julie, what are you doing? You think there's more water where that came from?"

She just glared at him. "I don't care," she almost screamed. "I was thirsty!"

James took a couple of strides back to Julie, and she cringed like she was afraid he was going to hit her. He didn't say a word; just stepped past her and picked up the plastic bottle and the cap that she had dropped. He took off his pack and put the empty capped bottle inside. Then he took out his own water bottle and, deliberately so she would watch, very carefully took a small sip of his own water. He then returned his water bottle to his pack and put the pack back on, before very calmly saying, "let's go."

They hadn't taken more than a couple of steps when they heard what had to be machine gun fire off in the distance ahead of them. Then they felt, as much as heard, a single loud blast, like a bomb exploding. A black cloud of smoke started rising; it looked to be coming from up the interstate, a mile or so ahead of them. They watched the smoke rise straight up for a few hundred feet, then, catching a breeze aloft, stream off toward the mountains in the west. Next, came the rumbling sound of another convoy of some kind. It was coming toward them from the north; from the location of the explosion. James looked around for a place to hide. For some reason, he had a fear of whatever was heading their way. He grabbed Julie and pulled her into the shallow ditch on the east side of the interstate.

"Down in the ditch. Hurry!" He didn't really wait for her to get down, but instead pulled her.

"Ouch!" her knees hit the gravel harder than James intended. "Goddamn it, James, you're hurting me."

Ignoring her complaints, he ordered her to lie down at the same time as he pulled her on down into the ditch. "Don't move, they'll just think we're more dead people," he whispered as if the people in the approaching vehicles could hear them.

James had positioned himself so he could peer over the edge of the road to get a look at whatever it was coming from the north on the other side of I-25. It wasn't what he thought it was at all. The vehicles producing the loud rumbling weren't in any way similar to the convoys they'd heard and seen before. James didn't know much of anything about military hardware, but he knew enough to see that what was rumbling down the interstate was a convoy consisting of just two tanks of some kind. The lead tank had a bulldozer type blade in front with some kind of large gun above the blade. The second tank didn't have a blade, but it had an equally large gun; the gun on the second tank was pointed back up the highway from where they'd come. The tanks must not have been autonomous since they didn't have an antennae truck leading them. They must have had some kind of connection to each other, though; they continued heading south down the interstate, perfectly maintaining no more than a tank's length between them. As they passed by, James regretted having basically thrown Julie into the ditch. Whoever was in those tanks, they would have probably just ignored James and Julie, anyway.

His knees hurt where they had hit the gravel. Looking down, he could see that the knees of his jeans were bloody. Then he looked at Julie. She was now sitting up, holding her bent knees in her hands. She was crying, and when she reached up to brush the tears away, her hand had blood on it, as well. He sat beside her and put his arm around her shoulder.

"I'm sorry, Julie. I didn't mean to hurt you. I was trying to protect you." He pulled her close and she didn't resist; she just started sobbing harder. "When I heard the explosion, it just freaked me out. How are we supposed to know what or who's safe, and what isn't?" he tried to soothe her.

"God, I'm scared," she managed to get out between sobs. "Where are we going? What are we going to do?"

For several minutes, James just held her, letting her sob it out of her system. Then, when the sobbing stopped, he got a bag of the trail mix and some jerky out of his pack and offered some to her. "We just have to get home," he said. "We'll be safe there."

The trail mix was stale, and the jerky had long ago passed its sell by date, but both of them were hungry enough that it was definitely better than nothing. James offered Julie some of his water to wash down the nuts and dried fruit. She accepted, and very carefully only drank about half of what was left in the bottle. That left James a couple of swallows and then they were officially out of water. He rummaged around in his pack to see what else he had. It had been so long since he had used the pack that he couldn't remember what was in it. He felt something that was fairly bulky in its own nylon bag. Pulling it out, he remembered it. It was an old-fashioned water purification pump. He carefully put the water purifier back in his pack, relieved that maybe they could find some water after all. All they had to do was find a stream or pond that hadn't dried up, and they could refill their water bottles.

The sun was getting pretty low in the western sky. James gave Julie a hug and asked her if she was okay to walk some more. They both had sore knees, but managed to start walking again, headed toward the smoke that was still rising from something a mile or so up the interstate.

The smoke had all but died out completely by the time they got to the scene of destruction. It looked like it had been a convoy of some kind in its own right. There were the blackened remains of what appeared to be one of the light armored vehicles they'd seen earlier, along with one of the antennae carrying vehicles, but what really caught James attention, was the remains of the third vehicle in the convoy. It was an autonomous armored stretch limo, like the one his dad preferred to travel in. There wasn't much left of the limo. It looked like it had been hit with some kind of armor piercing projectile that had then exploded, blowing it open from the inside out. Another light armored vehicle had been bringing up the rear. It hadn't suffered as much damage as the others, but it was full of holes. James surmised that it must have been hit by the machine gun fire they'd heard. The bullets must have been armor piercing as well. All of the vehicles had been pushed into the median, between the two halves of the interstate. *Must be what the dozer blade on the tank was for,* James thought. He had a strong foreboding feeling, as he stopped to ponder the scene of destruction. Other than the light armored vehicles appearing to be military, this could have easily been the kind of secure motorcade that his father usually traveled in.

Julie silently surveyed the scene as well. It was hard to tell what her thoughts might be. She had to be thinking about her mother, James concluded. Her mother had, no doubt always traveled with a military escort. Their silent reverie was shattered by two fighter drones that screamed overhead no more than fifty feet above them. The roar of their engines hitting James and Julie a few seconds after the drones were already gone. It couldn't have been more than a few more seconds before they heard two explosions from the south, back toward Colorado Springs. There was no way to know for sure, but James had a feeling that the drones had just taken out the two tanks they'd seen earlier. He had the unsettling thought that it really was some kind of revolution. There wasn't much doubt left that some part of the military was now pitted against some other part. *Dr. Mitchell was right,* James thought. *The revolution he predicted must be happening.* He wondered again what had happened to John Mitchell, and the other students and faculty from Colorado College.

The sun was starting to drop behind the mountains to the west and Ken's words came back to James. *What had he meant about it not being safe to travel at night?* It didn't seem to be safe to travel, period; but he now had a nagging feeling that they needed to take cover somewhere. A short way ahead of them, he could see some cottonwood trees on either side of the interstate; a meandering line of trees stretching out to the east and the west that had to be a stream, or at least a creek bed. He didn't say anything at all to Julie, just started walking again. He had made up his mind to get off of I-25. He had decided that they should follow the creek line to the east; maybe they could find some water and a place to hole up for the night.

Chapter 12

They reached the outskirts of Castle Rock at mid-morning on their fourth day of walking. They had worked their way north on back roads and old highways on the east side of I-25. It had taken longer than James thought it would, but they had continued to hide every night. James was never sure what or who it was that they were hiding from, but he decided it was better to be safe than dead. There had been the sound of explosions off in the distance every day. *Must be what it's like in a war zone,* James had thought, before realizing that they actually were in some kind of a war zone.

Fortunately, there had been plenty of places to fill their water bottles. As they crossed mostly dried up streams and creeks, there always seemed to be a few pockets of water, even in the creeks that had completely dried up. Finding food was another matter, though. They had finished the last of the jerky and trail mix by nightfall of the second day. Neither James nor Julie had eaten anything for a day and a half by the time they got to Castle Rock. They had passed by several farms and seen quite a few people, but no one was willing to share any food. Some were probably as hungry as James and Julie, and the rest were jealously guarding whatever food they had.

It seemed that the people out away from the cities had all banded together into groups that were protecting whatever supplies and meager farm crops they might have. Every time James and Julie passed one of the farms where the groups were gathered, there would be a number of armed people guarding their perimeter. None of them actually threatened James and Julie with violence, but they also made it abundantly clear that they should just keep moving. The farms and houses that weren't protected by armed guards had all been totally abandoned by people and animals alike. James had searched a couple of the empty places, looking for something to eat, but the places he searched had already been stripped bare of pretty much everything.

Julie's cough was getting worse. James stopped walking when he heard the hacking rasp of her cough too far behind him. It seemed like she had been getting slower and slower, as her cough got worse. He had first noticed that she seemed ill yesterday afternoon. She had spent the previous night snuggled up to James, shivering, even though the temperature didn't drop below about eighty degrees. *I'm not feeling the best, either,* he thought, as he turned to wait for Julie to catch up. He felt light-headed and weak. It seemed like his whole body ached. If he hadn't started coughing a little bit himself, he would have just blamed it on hunger and exhaustion; but it was beginning to feel like descriptions he'd heard of the flu or something. He didn't understand how they could have the flu; everyone he knew, and especially everyone at Colorado College, had received the universal flu vaccine. The flu was supposed to be something from the past, like small-pox or polio, or some of the other diseases that had been eradicated years ago. *So, if it isn't the flu, what is it?*

"Are you okay?" he asked Julie when she caught up to him.

"I don't know," she said. "I've never felt like this before." She was overcome by another coughing fit before she could say anything else.

James took his pack off and got out some water. He offered her the water, thinking maybe it would help relieve her cough. She took a few sips of the water, which did seem to bring her some relief.

"You don't need to save water now," he told her. "It's only a few more miles." He looked around at the houses that now lined both sides of the street they were on. Most looked deserted, but there were a few, here and there, that looked like they might still be occupied. *Maybe I should see if anyone will give us something to eat,* he thought. *Not very likely,* he decided. He thought about searching through the abandoned looking places, but that, too, seemed futile. All of the places he'd searched before had turned up empty.

He decided that it wouldn't hurt to try one of the houses that looked occupied. Feeling the weight of the pistol that he still carried stuffed into the waistband of his jeans, the thought occurred to him that anyone in any of those houses was probably armed, and he probably better make damn sure they didn't think he was a threat. He took the pistol out of his pants and stuck it in his pack. He took another look around, and not seeing anyone anywhere, told Julie to wait here by the pack.

"Where are you going?" she asked.

"I just want to see if anyone's home," he replied, and headed across the street toward an older brick house that still had all of its doors and windows intact. He walked straight up the sidewalk to the front door, with just a tinge of fear that someone might just shoot first and ask questions later. He stood in front of the door for a moment, listening. The only sounds he could hear were the scattered sounds of birds in the immediate neighborhood. There were no sounds at all coming from the house. He rapped his knuckles on the old wooden front door and waited. The house remained totally silent. Knocking harder and louder at the door, he yelled, "anyone home?" Still no answer.

Pondering just what he should do now, he reached down and tried the latch. The door was locked. He didn't dare break in, there was probably someone on the other side of the door with a gun, just waiting to blast anyone who might try that. He had just decided that it was no use; that no one was going to help them, and started to turn away when he heard what sounded like a moan coming from inside the house. "Hello," he shouted. "Can you help us?" More silence was the only answer he got from inside.

James looked both ways, up and down the street, wondering if anyone had heard him. Wondering, for that matter, if there really was anyone on this street at all. Julie, who had now sat down on the curb where he had left her, was the only person in sight. He decided to go around to the back of the house. He walked around the side of the house to where he'd seen a gate in the fenced back yard. Inside the gate, the back yard was nothing but dirt. What had once been a lawn had dried up long ago. The front yard had been covered with gravel at some point, in an effort at landscaping, but the backyard had simply been allowed to die out and return to bare dirt.

The fence was about halfway from the front of the house to the back, so, as he walked past, James tried looking in the side windows on the inside of the fence. The windows on this side were completely covered with some kind of drapes, just as the windows on the front side had been. He started getting a whiff of a bad smell just as he went through the gate, and coming around the back corner of the house, the smell just about gagged him. He recognized the smell from the corpses they'd walked by on their way up from Colorado Springs. Just as he realized what the smell was, he saw the source. The house had a covered concrete patio that was raised up above the yard by a couple of feet, probably at the same level as the floor of the house. The corpse was sprawled down the steps leading up to the patio. It appeared to be a man. Thankfully, it was lying face down, so James didn't have to look at whatever was left of the face.

He heard another moaning sound, and, trying to ignore the corpse as much as possible, walked around the body to investigate. The back door of the house was standing ajar with swarms of flies buzzing in and out. James could see what must have been hundreds of them crawling all over the dead man. The moaning sound was definitely coming from inside the house. James wanted to go in; maybe he could help someone. Maybe he could find something to eat. The thought of something to eat, combined with the smell coming out of the house and off of the dead body lying on the stairs, caused him to wretch. He heaved and lost what little bit of water he'd just had to drink. There was nothing else to throw up. *I can't.* The thought turned him back away from the patio. *What could I do to help, anyway?* He dry-heaved some more as he stumbled back around the corner of the house and headed back across the street. *We can get home,* he thought. *We don't need any help.*

James knew they would have to cross I-25 in order to get home to Castle Pines. He was dreading that part, wondering if they should wait until nightfall to try to sneak across in the dark. That wasn't going to work. He was helping Julie every step of the way now. He held her left arm around his shoulder and had his right arm around her waist as they trudged up the deserted four-lane street toward the I-25 interchange. When they got close enough to see the interstate, James was surprised to see a few vehicles traveling across the overpass. As they got closer, he was even more surprised to see that it wasn't just military convoys like they'd seen back at Colorado Springs. Though there weren't nearly as many vehicles as there should have been, it seemed to be somewhat normal traffic; mostly trucks, but one or two passenger vehicles as well. They definitely had military escorts, but he couldn't see any of the vehicles with dish antennas. He had the sudden realization that Amerinet and the GPS and communication networks must be back up and functioning.

Damn – wish I had my com, he thought, as they got closer to the interchange. The interchange was barricaded off with military personnel and various armored vehicles and tanks blocking the entrance to I-25. There were also freight vans and water tankers parked under the overpass bridges. There was a banner of some kind above the barricades, but James couldn't make out what it said. When they got closer, he could see a group of people walking down the exit ramp off of I-25 headed toward the military encampment. At about the same time, he was able to read the banner. It said: *U.S. ARMY - REFUGEE AID STATION.*

"Look! We're safe now." His voice was hoarse, and the words were followed by another cough. A deep rasping cough was the only reply he got from Julie.

So, the country was still functioning. James was so relieved at first that he failed to notice that all of the army personnel were wearing masks. When he did notice, he was shocked to see that they weren't just some kind of filter masks; everyone was wearing a minimum of what looked like full-fledged gas masks. Many of the troops were not only wearing gas masks but were covered from head to toe in white hazmat suits. Wondering just what would cause the soldiers to be wearing hazmat suits, James half-dragged a stumbling Julie toward the checkpoint entrance to the aid station. *Damn, that's gotta be hot,* he thought, as he approached the fully covered soldier at the entrance.

The soldier at the checkpoint was a woman, her voice muffled by the hood and full-face mask she was wearing. "Where are you from?" she asked, temporarily barring their entrance to the aid station. "Do you have some I.D.?"

Normally, James would have used his com for identification, and he felt a bit of panic that the soldier wouldn't help them; then he remembered his billfold was in the bottom of his pack. Unlike the military units that had attacked the college and seemed to be running Colorado Springs, James had an immediate trust of the troops at this aid station. Without knowing how he knew, he just knew that these people were regular army, and they were definitely not part of whatever revolutionary force it was they had escaped from. "I'm James Mendez," he told the soldier, as he took off his backpack. Another cough wracked his chest before he could add, "and this is Julie Johnson." There was no recognition in the eyes of the soldier, as James handed her his autonomous vehicle operator's license. "Robert Mendez is my father, and Julie is the daughter of Senator Jill Johnson."

The soldier looked at the ID, then back at James and Julie. Her eyes got wide as she realized they truly were who he said they were. "Come with me," she said, motioning another soldier to take her place at the check station. She led them back into the center of the camp, which was quite a bit bigger than James had first thought. There were tents and trailers set up underneath the overpass bridges of I-25, with more temporary barracks, tanks, and all kinds of armored vehicles stretching out into the flat area on the west side of the interchange. She led James and Julie to a large white trailer that had a big red cross on the side. The inside of the trailer looked like an old-fashioned doctor's office on one end, but the rest of the trailer looked like something out of a bad apocalyptic movie. There was a hallway going down one side of the trailer with hospital beds lining the other side. James quickly counted the beds; there were twenty, and all but two were empty. The two closest to the office each had people in them. Both patients were wearing oxygen masks and had IV drips set up beside them.

The soldier bent down to tell the woman at the desk something, and James noticed that this woman, who was obviously a doctor, wasn't wearing a mask at all. The doctor stood up and started around the desk just as James felt Julie go limp, leaving him to support her full weight. A nurse, who was wearing a mask, saw Julie faint and rushed over to help. "Get her to number three," the doctor ordered leading the way and pulling the cover down from the third bed. With help from the nurse, James was able to get Julie onto the hospital bed, before having a coughing fit himself that left him feeling dizzy and lightheaded.

"You better take this bed," the doctor told him. He sat down on the bed next to Julie's.

He watched as the nurse and doctor worked together getting an oxygen mask on Julie and some kind of IV drip started into her arm. The two hardly spoke, but their movements were smooth and coordinated; a choreographed routine that they had obviously practiced many times.

"What's wrong with her?" he asked the doctor while suppressing a cough.

Finished with Julie, at least for the time being, the doctor turned to James. "She's been infected with V1, I'm sure, and so have you, I think," she told him. The questioning look in his eyes let her know that he had no idea what she was talking about. "It's a virus. A very dangerous virus that I'm sure you have never heard of. Now, let me look at you." With that, she pointed a thermometer into his ear. "Only a hundred and one," she said, almost to herself, as she attached the device to his left index finger that would tell her his pulse rate and blood oxygen levels.

"V1 is extremely contagious and very deadly," she told James, as she studied the monitor by the side of the bed. "The government has been suppressing any information about the virus to prevent panic. We think it came here from Europe, but some CDC scientists are speculating that it is some kind of ancient pathogen that was released by the thawing of the permafrost in Siberia." She turned from looking at the monitor and looked at James. "You should know that this virus, V1, has a very high mortality rate." She kept her voice perfectly flat, studying his eyes for reaction to what she had just said.

The nurse brought a glass of some kind of thick orange liquid and handed it to James. No one had to say anything, his hunger was overpowering. He drained the glass slowly, letting it soothe his throat as it filled his shrunken stomach. It tasted of orange juice and medicine. Had he not been starving, he would have thought it undrinkable. As it was, it seemed delicious.

"She'll be alright now, though?" he asked as he set the glass on the bedside table. "Now that she's getting treatment."

The doctor sort of slumped and almost imperceptibly shook her head from side to side. "I'm not sure," she told him honestly. "Maybe if we had the right antiviral… all we can do now is treat the symptoms and hope for the best."

It suddenly occurred to James that Julie wasn't the only one he should be worried about. He already felt better after drinking the orange concoction, but the doctor had said that he, too, had been infected. And what about the doctor, herself? "Why aren't you wearing a mask, like the others?" he asked her directly.

"I seem to be immune," she said, studying James to gauge his reaction. "Not just me," she said. "I believe you are also immune. I should say, I believe our immune systems are somehow able to fight off the virus." She seemed to focus somewhere beyond James. "I don't know why. If only…"

An alarm went off on the display that was above the first bed in the room. The doctor jolted out of her reverie, turned and, along with the nurse, went over to that bedside. She reached up and turned off the alarm. The nurse methodically removed the oxygen mask from the patient's face and the IV from her arm. There was nothing urgent in their movements; just the same routine they had practiced far too many times before. The doctor pulled a com out of a pocket in her uniform and spoke a few words into it, while the nurse pulled the sheet up over the patients face. James watched silently as they carefully rolled the dead young woman up in the sheet that had been covering her. Two soldiers dressed in hazmat suits came through the door with a stretcher, and without saying a word, rolled the sheet wrapped body onto the stretcher and carried it out. The doctor still had a kind of faraway look in her eyes, and James could see through her face mask that the nurse was crying.

"Was that one of the refugees?" he asked, without really directing the question at either one of them.

"No," the doctor answered, "that was Shandy. She was a nurse. We've stopped trying to save any of the refugees."

James looked around the room; at the doctor and nurse who seemed to both be in a mild state of shock, at Julie lying on a hospital bed with an IV drip and an oxygen mask, at the only other patient, a middle-aged man who was also wearing an oxygen mask and had an IV drip beside his bed. Both patients were unconscious. "What about him?" James asked gesturing toward the other patient. "Is he a soldier, then?"

The doctor seemed to snap out of it and looked at James with a sad smile. "No," she said, "not a soldier. That's Tom. Doctor Thomas Welch. He's in," she corrected herself, "he was in charge of this facility."

The nurse's shoulders were shaking as she looked down at the unconscious doctor. Her silent sobs betraying the depths of her grief. James felt her grief. He was becoming overcome with grief, himself; not wanting to admit the truth that he knew instinctively. He looked at the doctor and asked, "Does anyone recover?"

The doctor looked down at the floor, and quietly said, "Just a few, like you and me."

James' mind was racing. The doctor had said that Julie needed an anti-viral that obviously was not available. Maybe his dad could get some. "Call my father, maybe he can get you some of the anti-viral drugs."

The com in the doctor's pocket buzzed. She listened to it for just a few seconds, then placed it back in her pocket. "That was Captain Rogers. They've been trying to reach your father since you arrived. They can't get through."

James started to protest, "what do you mean, they can't get through? Who did they talk to? Let me borrow your com, they'll let me talk to him."

The doctor was shaking her head as she took the com out of her pocket and offered it to James. "Have it call the MICI home office," he told her, knowing that it would probably only obey her commands. She did as he requested and handed him the com. James put the com to his ear and listened for the fake ringing sound that was a carryover from the age of the telephone. The com clicked like it was starting to ring, and the line went dead. *What the hell,* he thought. James took the com away from his ear and looked at it like maybe he could figure out what was wrong if he stared at it long enough. *Why did I leave my com?* He berated himself. If he only had his com, he could call home or even Robert's personal com. It was impossible with a stranger's com, though. Even if he knew the right number or code, neither of his parent's coms would allow incoming calls from unknown sources.

The doctor reached out and gently took the com out of his hand. "It probably wouldn't make any difference anyway," she said. The resignation in her voice was chilling.

"What do you mean it wouldn't make any difference?" James almost yelled at her, frustration starting to get the best of him. "You said they need an anti-viral." He looked at the two patients; one a doctor that he didn't know, and Julie. Julie who had let him lead her here to this place. She'd trusted him to take care of her. He knew that she loved him in her own way, and he couldn't help but feel love for her as well. Love, and a responsibility to protect her.

The doctor looked away from James and said simply, "Dr. Welch had an anti-viral." She went on to explain that they had arrived at this camp with several doses of an experimental anti-viral drug that they thought would combat the virus. At first, they'd used it on the refugees that came in sick. It seemed like it was working, so they sent out an order for more. It was just about then that the world turned upside down. The tsunami hit Washington at just about the same time as the revolution hit the military. The first of the refugees they'd treated with the anti-viral had seemed to get well, only to relapse within a couple of days. All had died. Even though the doctors and nurses had all followed proper protocols, they too, began to get sick.

Dr. Martin had been one of the first to start feeling ill. She'd tried to hide it from the rest of them. She said it had affected her much like it seemed to be affecting James. She'd had a mild fever for a couple of days and felt a little weak and light headed, but then it had passed. Then it hit Dr. Welch. Knowing that they had no alternative, even though it hadn't saved anyone yet, they administered the last dose of the anti-viral to him. Just like the others, he seemed to get well but then relapsed two days later. He'd been lying here in a coma since yesterday. "He'll be gone before nightfall..." she trailed off into silence.

The muffled sound of a cough broke the silence, and James was startled when he realized that it wasn't Julie or Dr. Welch. It was the nurse that had been crying. The sound of her coughing was muffled by the mask she wore. James had a sudden overwhelming desire to flee, to just get away. *This was no aid station; it was a death camp. But what about Julie?* He couldn't just leave her here. He had to get help. "I'll go for help," he said as he stood up to leave.

The nurse sat down on the bed where another nurse had just died and slowly reached up and removed her mask. Her face was still streaked with tears, but she was no longer crying. She'd resigned herself to her fate. "There is no help," she said softly.

At first, Captain Rogers had been reluctant to give James any assistance at all. After getting one of the soldiers who was posted outside the infirmary to take him to whoever was in charge, James had asked for a ride into Denver to try to find his dad. The captain had told him that the rebels had hit Denver pretty hard, and there wasn't much left of the downtown business district. It seemed that the rebel's main purpose had been to attack the centers of business and finance; to hit the wealthy elite establishment as hard as they could while doing as little damage as possible to the lower rungs of society. James had the uneasy feeling that the Captain was somewhat ambivalent about the rebellion; that he sympathized with the cause, even if he couldn't bring himself to support it openly. Captain Rogers had also been concerned about the number of troops that were deserting. It seemed that everyone wanted to get away from the camp, as if getting away would do them any good. He'd finally relented and agreed to have a trusted lieutenant drive James the few miles to his parent's home in Castle Pines.

The lieutenant, dressed in a full hazard protection suit, didn't seem to want to talk at all as he "drove" James out of the camp. They were in one of the autonomous light armored vehicles, so the lieutenant didn't really drive the vehicle; he simply told the vehicle where to go. It was a pretty secure system. Once the vehicle was assigned to the driver or vice versa, the vehicle would only function on the driver's commands.

Looking out through the small horizontal slits that served as the only windows in the vehicle, James noticed that there didn't seem to be as many soldiers as when they'd arrived, just an hour or two earlier. *If they're deserting that fast,* he thought, *the camp will be empty in no time.* He was musing on that as they left the camp, headed north and west. What he saw next was the most shocking thing he'd seen in the last few days, maybe the most shocking thing he'd ever seen. They were passing a large pit that had been recently excavated just a short way from the camp. There were a couple of military dump trucks backed up to the edge of the pit. At first, James couldn't tell what they were dumping into the pit, and then he realized they were bodies. All kinds of dead bodies; still dressed in whatever they'd been wearing when they died. Some were obviously refugees or homeless people, but there were others, as well. There were even what appeared to be soldiers among the bodies; still wearing the hazmat gear that had not protected them. As they passed the pit, the scope of the crisis hit James like a sledgehammer. There were bodies piled on bodies. Hundreds, maybe thousands. It was like nature had given up on humankind and decided to just wipe the species off the face of the earth. *And why not,* he thought. *How many species have we driven to extinction?* The rest of the short trip to the place in Castle Pines that he'd always known as home was a time for silent reflection. It seemed that mother earth or nature had declared war on mankind. But then again, it was really the other way around. Man had long ago declared war on nature. He thought about how fast, in the greater scheme of things, man had destroyed so much. He knew from his studies of recent history how people had been warned a long time ago of the consequences of their actions. One of the things that had most interested James about the effects of climate change had been how much faster devastation had hit than the scientists of the late twentieth and early twenty-first centuries had predicted it would. Twenty years ago, they had predicted at most a few feet of sea level rise by the end of the century. In the twenty short years since those predictions, the great ice sheets had melted much faster than predicted. Sea level was more than a meter higher now than it had been at the dawn of the twenty-first century.

James' musings on man and nature were interrupted by the lieutenant. "Shit!" The exclamation was muffled by the hazmat mask and hood that completely covered the lieutenants head. The vehicle came to a sudden stop as the muffled voice continued, "nav-net's down again. I knew we should have used one of the antique Humvees. Shit," he exclaimed again for emphasis.

James, looking through the small window, recognized the familiar neighborhood. They were only about a half mile from home. He could faintly hear some kind of communication coming through the lieutenant's hood. The hazmat suits had coms built in. At least coms are still working, he thought. "I'll walk the rest," he told the lieutenant, who was listening closely to whatever was coming through his com. The lieutenant seemed to ignore him, so he pulled the emergency exit latch and pushed the gull-wing door up and out of his way. He stepped out, closed the door and started walking as fast as he could up the hill toward home. He had one driving thought, *Julie will die if I don't get her better treatment than what they have at that aid station. Dad's doctors will surely have the right anti-viral. If? If…?* The thought was left hanging as he got to the top of the hill.

The view from this spot had always been one of James' favorites, especially at night. From this point most of the greater Denver area filled the vista to the north; the high-rise buildings in the distance marking downtown Denver, itself. James stopped and stared, having trouble comprehending what his eyes were seeing. The high-rise buildings of downtown Denver were gone. All that he could see were a few wisps of smoke still rising from where downtown Denver should have been. From this distance, he could only imagine what the piles of rubble must look like where the skyscrapers had once stood. The MICI building had been one of those skyscrapers that were no longer there.

Chapter 13

The Mendez estate was surrounded by a rock wall, whose purpose of providing security was expertly camouflaged by the sheer beauty of the stonework. It had been constructed by true artisans using a massive amount of native stone. The only opening in the twenty-foot-high wall was where the split driveways accessed the property. There was a large guardhouse between the entrance and exit drives with wrought iron looking gates across both. The gates were designed to look like oversize ornamental wrought iron, but they were actually constructed of very heavy-duty steel. The gates and the guard house were only about half as tall as the wall, but James knew the guard house was always manned, with at least six people who were armed well enough to defend it against any attack, even an attack by a tank.

As he approached, James could see the sun glistening off of the one-way bullet-proof glass wall of the guardhouse that faced the road. He expected to see the door in the side of the guardhouse, which was inside the gate, opening at any moment. Surely, they wouldn't recognize him in his current state. Protocol required one guard to come out into the open to confront any approaching stranger, while the others manned the armaments that would be aimed at any potential threat. Knowing the guns that would be aimed at him through the small openings in the façade gave James a little bit of a chill as he approached the gate.

He walked right up to the gate and still no one came out of the guardhouse. Now that he was this close, he could see through the steel bars of the gate that the door into the guardhouse was slightly ajar. A shiver of fear ran up his spine. "Hey!" he yelled. "It's James. Anybody home?" The eerie silence that answered filled him with more foreboding than anything he had ever experienced.

There was no way to open the gates manually from the outside. The estate had its own electric power, generated by wind and sun, and enough battery backup to get through any period of non-generation, but there had never been a mechanism to activate the gates from the outside. Security concerns had trumped any inconvenience of not being able to control the gates from the outside, and the entrance was guarded around the clock; until now, that is. *Now what?* James looked at the gates and yelled as loud as he could at the empty driveway that led through the trees toward the house. None of the buildings of the estate were visible from here, but his voice should carry that far. He yelled again. Still nothing. He looked the gate up and down and started climbing. He remembered that Robert's chief of security had wanted to electrify the gates, but his mother had put her foot down. "It's too much like a prison, already," he remembered her saying. *Good thing she got her way that time,* he thought, as he reached the top and swung his leg over to the other side.

"Hold it right there." James froze, one leg on one side of the gate and one on the other; astraddle the big iron bars like the gate was some kind of mechanical horse. He looked up to see a man with an assault rifle coming toward him from the edge of the trees along the driveway. It was Don. "Don, thank God; it's me, James."

Don helped James get down off of the gate. They looked each other up and down. Don looked like he always had, clean shaven, muscular, well dressed; but now his clothes and hands were dirty. The main difference James noticed, though, was the haunted look in Don's eyes, as he grabbed James and gave him a bear-hug.

"Goddamn, James. It's good to see you." He let go of the hug and held James out at arm's length. "You look like hell."

James tried not to breathe. Don shouldn't be touching him. He pushed Don away and turned his head before saying, "Don, I'm contagious. Back away – please. It's terrible."

Don's response was not to back away at all. Instead, he laughed. There was a kind of madness in his laughter that shook James somewhere deep inside. "You think you're the only one?" he got out between his laughter. Laughter that now seemed to be only about half laughter and half crying. "Where do you think the others are?" he asked, motioning toward the guardhouse. "They're dead! That's where they are James. They're all dead. I just finished burying Sam. He was the last one. Hell, I buried them all."

Don got himself under control and retrieved the assault rifle from where he'd leaned it against the side of the guardhouse. "Come on," he said, latching the guardhouse door. "Boy, is Noni going to be glad to see you."

His mother was alive. A wave of relief swept over James. "What about Dad?" he asked, as they hurried up the drive towards the house.

Don stopped so he could look at James to give him the news. "We honestly don't know for sure; but James, I'm afraid he's gone. He was at the office when the missiles hit. At least that's where he was last I knew. I'm sorry James."

The news didn't really surprise James, but it shocked him, none the less. Don started walking again. "That's why your Mom is going to be so glad to see you," he added as if to get James to hurry. As they hurried to the house, Don told him that his father had known something was going on between different factions in the military establishment. He'd received a warning of some kind from one of the defense contractors that a substantial minority of people throughout the military were talking about taking the country back from the wealthy. Robert's source had feared that it would come to some kind of violence, if not full out revolution. So, he'd sent Don and a security detail to go to Colorado Springs to get James. The security detail had been headed south on I-25 less than a mile north of the Castle Pines Parkway exit when their convoy of autonomous vehicles died, and the missiles started hitting Denver. It was extremely lucky that they were as close to Castle Pines as they were. They'd abandoned their vehicles and made their way home on foot. "Some of them were already sick, though," Don said. Then, almost as an afterthought, "sick with what? What kind of sickness kills so many people so fast? Was it some kind of germ warfare? What the hell is it?"

James didn't have a chance to respond. They were walking again and had reached the front of the house when Noni Mendez came running out the front door. She must have been watching through the window. There were tears in both their eyes when James and his mother threw their arms around each other and just held on tight. Words were unnecessary, and the silent embrace lasted long enough for Don to walk over and sit down on the step.

The mix of emotions was overwhelming for James. The utter relief of finding his mother okay mixed with the sorrow of finding out that his father was probably dead. On top of the sorrow at the loss of his father, he had a profound sense of guilt. Over the past several years, James had come to believe that he hated his father for so thoroughly controlling his life. Now he felt guilty. His father had only ever wanted what was best for him, how could he have rejected that? And now, there would never be a reconciliation. His father was gone; gone forever. So much was gone; so many people who were now gone forever.

Still holding his mother as tight as he could, his thoughts turned to Julie. She wasn't gone. At least, not yet. "Mother, do you know if Dr. Yew is…is still alive?" It seemed so strange to be asking if a fixture of their lives was still among the living. Dr. Yew had been the Mendez family doctor since before James was born. And Dr. Yew was not just an ordinary family doctor. He was a leading research physician, with connections to everything from the Mayo Clinic to the Centers For Disease Control. If anyone would know of anything to help Julie, it would be Dr. Yew.

Noni Mendez let go of her son and held him out where she could look at him. "James, are you sick?" The question was edged with fear that went way beyond concern.

"No, not me," he answered quickly to relieve her anxiety. "I mean, I have been. Some. But I think I'm immune. It's Julie. Julie's the one who's…" he couldn't bring himself to say dying, "sick. She needs some kind of antiviral." Even as he said it, he had another concern. "What about you Mom? Are you okay?"

"I'm fine, James. At least I think I am. For some reason, whatever it is, it spared me. Me and Don." She looked away, as she added, "everyone else is gone. I'm afraid Dr. Yew might be gone, too. We tried to get him the day before yesterday when Sam and the others got so sick. We left messages on his com, but he never called back."

"We have to find him. Is the com working?" James was already ushering his mother back inside as he spoke. He went straight to the kitchen. He was still so hungry and thirsty that he was filling a water glass and looking for food, even as he commanded the house com to call Dr. Yew. There was no response from the house com. He tried again, as he rummaged through the kitchen grabbing some cheese and crackers. Still nothing.

"That's odd," Noni said. "I was just talking to Dad a few minutes ago."

"Damn! The net's down again," James managed, between mouthfuls of cheese and crackers. "Is Grandpa okay?" He hadn't thought about Grandpa Chuck much lately. Thinking about Grandpa Chuck and the BR always led to memories of Anna;

memories and feelings he tried to avoid. Memories and thoughts that were triggered, even now, by simply asking about his Grandpa. Sure, he was worried about Grandpa Chuck, but he really wanted to hear that Anna was okay. Thinking about Anna invariably led to more feelings of guilt. And now the guilt was double. He still felt terrible guilt for the way he'd discarded Anna's love, and now he felt another guilt for even thinking about Anna while Julie was dying in Castle Rock.

Noni told James that Grandpa Chuck had said he was fine, and that as far as he knew the sickness, whatever it was, had not even affected the western slope. He hadn't been to Kremmling in over a week, but everyone had seemed fine last time he was there.

Noni didn't mention Anna at all, but her words lifted a terrible weight off of James. *Maybe this sickness was local. Maybe the whole world isn't dying. There's still hope.* The feelings of hope for his grandpa and for Anna compounded his feelings of guilt over his relationship with Julie, and his feelings of grief, or guilt for a lack of grief, for the death of his father.

"I have to go." It was Don; the flat statement interrupting James' thoughts. "I have to get to Kansas City."

James remembered that Don was from Kansas City. He remembered him taking a few vacations to go back and spend time with his family.

"I have to know," Don went on. "I have to know, one way or another."

"I understand," James told him, and true understanding of just how much Don had sacrificed to look after his family hit James hard. Don was a friend as much as a Mendez family employee. How hard it must have been these past few days, protecting Noni while wondering about the well-being of his own mother.

"Have you heard anything from them?" James asked.

"Not since last week." Don seemed to be searching his memory, as he answered. "I tried calling as soon as the com came back online, but nothing. And now, coms out again. Who knows when, or if, they'll come back online?"

Torn between wanting Don to help him with Julie, and wanting to help Don find out about his own family, James decided the Mendez family had asked way too much of Don already. "You better take one of the old manuals," James told him, referring to the manually driven, non-autonomous, vehicles in Robert Mendez' private collection of automobiles. Don deserved anything James could give him.

Robert Mendez had been, among other things, a longtime collector of automobiles. The collection was housed in a long, low, warehouse that was architecturally designed to resemble an old-time riding stable. It was the largest building on the estate, and Noni had nicknamed it the car barn. The collection inside the car barn included everything from a fully restored Model T, to a 1964 Corvette, to the newest electric autonomous Rolls Royce.

Knowing that the only chance he had of saving Julie was to get her to a much better medical facility than the refugee aid station, James was as anxious to get going as Don was. He ushered Don out of the house, and they walked to the car barn together.

The new Rolls Royce had been delivered less than a month ago, and James was seeing it for the first time, as he and Don walked into the ornate, immaculately clean warehouse. The Rolls was a real beauty, but without the Navnet available for autonomous navigation it was basically little more than a sculptured work of art.

"Too bad you can't take the Rolls," James told Don. "Looks like she would have been a great way to travel."

"I wouldn't take that car even if I could," Don answered. "That's your Dad's favorite." James couldn't help but notice that Don had spoken of his father in the present, instead of the past.

"Take any of them you want," James said. "He owed you that. We owe you that."

Don decided that he'd better stick to one of the EVs since he had no idea if he'd be able to get gas or diesel anywhere between Denver and Kansas City. He ended up choosing the 2021 Rivian pickup. With its extra battery pack in the bed, it was probably the only one in the collection with enough range to get to Kansas City without recharging. Finding a functional charge station along the way was as questionable as finding gas or diesel.

"Don, I don't know how to thank you," James stuck out his hand to shake. Don grabbed his hand and pulled him into a hug.

"Thank me for what, James? I was only doing my job."

Only doing his job, James thought, holding up his hand in a final wave, as the Rivian eased out the door. Both men knew they would probably never see each other again. Don had always done so much more than just "his job". James had the disheartening thought that losing Don might be worse than losing his own father.

James liked Don's choice of the Rivian pickup but decided he would rather take the other Rivian anyway, the SUV. He had to find medical help for Julie. Too many were lost, he wouldn't let the disease claim her, as well. He decided that he would have to take his mother with him, instead of leaving her there alone. Even if they couldn't find Dr. Yew, they'd surely be able to find help at the University Hospital in Aurora.

At first, Noni didn't like the idea of leaving the security of the estate. She especially didn't like it when James wanted to leave the front gate open because there was no way to open it from the outside. James acquiesced and had to climb over the gate from the inside, after parking the Rivian on the outside and closing and locking the gate. He'd just have to climb back over to open it, once they got back.

It was an eerie drive back to the refugee aid station at Castle Rock. The autonomous armored vehicle that had brought James home was still parked at the bottom of the hill, but there was no sign of the lieutenant. That's what was eerie, there was no sign of anyone. At least not until they got to I-25. The first body they came across was on the edge of the on-ramp. They saw several more on the short four-mile drive to the aid station. James couldn't help but wonder how many they didn't see. They had to work their way around several stalled or abandoned vehicles, both civilian and military; how many of them had dead bodies inside? How could there possibly be so much death? The first living person they saw was a single man walking north over on the other side of the interstate. He was wearing some kind of military uniform, but from this side of I-25 James couldn't tell the branch or the rank of the man. It did seem kind of strange that he wasn't in the military hazmat gear that everyone had been wearing at the aid center. Just as James was about to get to the aid station exit ramp, two antique Humvees came out of the on-ramp and headed south down the interstate. *How many? How many people had the ability to fight off the disease that seemed to be killing nearly everyone?*

It had only been a couple of hours since James left the refugee aid station, but the place had changed dramatically. The hustle and bustle of an active military operation was gone. The entire aid station seemed mostly deserted. With the Navnet down, the trucks and armored vehicles were stalled and stranded all over the place. One of the dump trucks that had been collecting the dead was parked where it had dumped its last load of bodies, its bed still up in the air. The dozers that were supposed to cover the bodies sat still and lifeless behind the huge piles of earth that had been excavated to make the burial pit. The outside temperature display on the Rivian dashboard showed ninety-seven degrees, and the smell of those rotting bodies was overpowering, even with the windows up and the AC keeping the interior of the Riv at a comfortable seventy-five. James switched the AC to recirculate the interior air, but the smell was already inside.

"My God!" Noni exclaimed when she saw the burial pit. She had known it was bad, but the sheer scale of the unfolding tragedy hadn't hit her until then. She put her hand over her mouth and simply stared in shock and horror, not even noticing the tears that were running down her cheeks.

James pulled up to the medical trailer where he had left Julie. He had to get her out of there. That was the thought that drove him. He had to get her out of this place of death. He had to get her over to University Hospital. Even as he thought about it, he had the near certainty that University Hospital would be as lifeless as this camp. *Surely not. Surely, there's a proper hospital functioning somewhere. Surely, someone, somewhere has a treatment for this terrible virus or whatever it is.*

He found Dr. Martin seated at her desk in the medical trailer. She was sitting stock still staring out the window at the stillness of the camp. "Where is everybody?" he asked her, heading toward the row of beds where Julie and the nurse were still the only occupants.

He heard Dr. Martin mumble, "gone", as he saw Julie in the bed where he'd left her. Her face was still covered with the oxygen mask and the IV was still attached to her arm, but something was wrong. She was totally still. He glanced over at the nurse in the other bed. She, too, was still and silent. Then he looked up at the displays of the life support mechanizations and realized they were turned off. The screens were black and as silent as the bodies lying in the beds below them. It hit him like a train; Julie was dead. She was gone. The form there in the bed no more Julie than the dead body of the nurse that lay in the other bed.

He collapsed onto the bed next to Julie's dead body and wept. *How could he have failed to protect her? How could the world be like this? So much death. So much death.* He was overwhelmed by guilt. Guilt for failing Julie, guilt for living such an elite life, and guilt for being alive at all. That was the gist of his despair. *How could he be alive, while almost everyone else was dead and dying?*

James didn't know how long he sat on the bed and wept, but finally he managed to rouse himself up from despair, like a drowning man surfacing for air. He wiped the tears off his face and decided that he still had to get Julie out of here. Even if it was only her dead body that remained, he wouldn't leave her here to rot. He pulled the oxygen mask off of her face and pulled off the tape holding the IV in her arm. It seemed odd, but when he pulled the IV needle out, there was practically no blood. A single small drop oozed out of the hole in her arm. That was it. He pulled the bedsheet over her head and wrapped her up in it as best he could. Then, he stooped down and lifted her cold body up, draping her over his shoulder like a sack of seed. He was shocked by his lack of strength. After the hungry trek from Colorado Springs and the ravages of the disease, he knew that Julie couldn't have weighed over a hundred pounds, but the last few days had taken a toll on James as well. He felt weak, but not so weak that he couldn't carry Julie's dead body.

As he passed Dr. Martin on his way out, she was still just sitting, staring out the window. She seemed almost catatonic, but then, just as he was stepping out the door, he heard her say, "He killed himself, you know."

James stopped in the doorway. "Who? Who killed himself?" he asked, thinking he already knew the answer.

"Captain Rogers," she answered. "Why would he do that? He was one of us. He was immune. Why would he kill himself?"

Knowing Dr. Martin didn't expect an answer, as if there was an answer, James went down the steps and gently placed Julie's body in the cargo compartment of the SUV. As he pulled away, Dr. Martin was still staring aimlessly out her window. He wondered what would become of her; more importantly, what would become of any of them. *What would become of the few who survived?* He looked at his mother, and the question became even more pronounced. She was sitting silently, staring straight ahead, seemingly at nothing, with the same near catatonic look on her face as the one Dr. Martin had.

"Mother," James desperately wanted someone to not be lost, "I want to bury her at home. Is that okay?"

The question did seem to snap Noni out of her reverie, at least somewhat. "That's fine James," she said, as if they were discussing a normal everyday decision about a simple matter. Then she added, "let's go get your father. We should bury him at home, too."

James didn't really think they had much chance of finding Robert's body, but instead of heading straight home, James drove toward downtown Denver. The soldier they'd seen earlier was still walking up I-25, and since he was the only other living person in sight, James decided to stop and talk to him. The soldier had a rifle slung over his shoulder, and though he seemed a little worried about the Rivian pulling up to a stop beside him, he didn't reach for his gun. That seemed like a good sign. The soldier was walking on the left shoulder of the highway, so James just rolled down his driver's side window, wondering what to say. Nothing that would have been normal even a few hours ago seemed appropriate. He was about to say, need a lift, but decided that seemed like a strange question. *Of course, he needs a lift. He's walking, isn't he?*

"Where you headed?" was the best James could come up with.

The soldier was a young man, about James' age and build. The uniform he was wearing was desert camo, and James could now see that he was a member of the U.S. Army. But James had no idea what rank the soldier was; just a private, he presumed, though he wouldn't know a private from a sergeant without being told. The soldier looked around like he wasn't sure any of this was real. "Guess I don't know exactly," he said. "Just away, I guess. I don't really have any specific destination in mind."

Noni sat quietly staring straight ahead as if the soldier didn't even exist; almost as if the vehicle were still moving along the highway, and she was watching where they were going. James decided that with so few people left alive, it would be best if those who were, helped each other out. "Want to go with us?" James asked. "I'm James Mendez, and this is my mother, Noni."

"Where are you going?" the soldier asked. "And why would I want to go?"

He had an instant liking for the soldier. "Guess I don't really know where we're going either, in the long run," he said. "But in the near-term, I could use some help finding my dad. We'd like to take him home for a proper burial."

"Finding one dead person among so many seems like a pretty tall order," the soldier replied. "You plan on looking at every dead body out here." The motion of his head indicated that he basically included the whole world in the "out here."

James could have almost laughed at the absurdity of the situation. He felt like he should wake from an apocalyptic nightmare and find that none of this was real, but he knew that wouldn't happen. It was an apocalyptic nightmare, alright, but he wasn't dreaming. It was real. "No," James said, "we're pretty sure we know where he died. Don't think it was the sickness that got him. Think it was the bombs."

"Missiles," the soldier corrected him. "It wasn't bombs, it was missiles. That asshole, General Korliss, and his stupid rebellion. Like we needed another civil war. Like America wasn't already screwed." It was obvious that he had not been one of those who had rebelled. He looked around some more, deciding. "Guess I might as well," he said. "Not like I've got other things to do." He opened the passenger door behind James and climbed in. "Corporal David Ortiz," he introduced himself, then added, "guess the corporal doesn't mean much anymore. Just call me Dave." Then, "you collecting dead people?" he asked, looking at the sheet wrapped body behind the seats.

James explained about Julie as he resumed driving toward the MICI building. He told Dave where they expected to find Robert's body, and Dave told him that he was wasting his time. The army had already pulled out any survivors and casualties that could be found without heavy equipment to dig through the rubble. "Are you really Robert Mendez' son," he asked. He obviously found it ironic that circumstances had led him from poverty to the army to riding in the same vehicle with one of the richest people on earth. But then circumstances were nothing like they used to be. Nothing at all.

Noni, who hadn't said a word, seemed to snap out of it, at least momentarily. "He is," she said proudly, as if being rich and powerful had any meaning left in this new world.

They were only able to get within eight blocks of what was left of the MICI building. The destruction of the downtown area of Denver had been total. Here at the edge of the devastation, some buildings were still standing, and others had collapsed or partially collapsed. Scattered debris blocked the streets. Farther in toward the center of the destruction, the scattered debris became mountains of rubble where skyscrapers had once dominated the skyline.

They hadn't been able to find Robert Mendez, of course. After seeing the mountains of rubble, and having no idea where his body might be buried underneath it all, they hadn't really even tried. Noni had insisted that they look, so they had climbed over and around and through the rubble to the place where the MICI building had once stood, and James and Dave had made a show of digging through the rubble by hand. The futility of the effort was so obvious that they had only moved a few pieces of the rubble before making their way back to the SUV, and heading back to the Mendez Estate.

Dave patted down the last of the dirt on Julies Grave. James was leaning on his shovel, looking over what had once been his mother's flower garden, but was now a makeshift cemetery. No wonder Don had been dirty and exhausted, James thought, looking at the six other graves where Don had buried the rest of the security detail by himself. He was glad that Dave had agreed to help bury Julie. It had been a lot of work, even for the two of them.

"Do you want to pray, or something?" Dave, who was now also leaning on his shovel, asked.

"Pray for what?" James answered. "Pray that there's a God somewhere that can fix all of this? Do you believe in God, Dave? What kind of God would allow this to happen?"

"Yeah, not exactly the rapture that my folks expected, is it?" Dave said, looking up at the clear evening sky. "Guess it's Armageddon alright, but I don't think the righteous were spared any more than anyone else."

James wondered how many people, righteous or otherwise, actually had been spared. They had seen a few more living people on their way back to the estate from downtown Denver, but not many. James hadn't stopped to talk to any of them. What good would it have done? Did anyone who was still alive know why they didn't get sick and die along with everyone else? Did anyone have any idea how a virus or bacteria or whatever "it" was could have wiped out everyone in the span of just a few days? It was incomprehensible.

"So, your parents are religious?" James asked, just to make conversation.

"Were," Dave answered. "My parents were religious. Extremely religious. Or, at least, that's how I remember them. They were killed in the border riots of twenty-six." He grew pensive for a moment, then; "Kind of ironic, isn't it? I've spent most of the last two years keeping people just like them from coming across that same border. Guess it doesn't really matter anymore though, does it?"

There wasn't much that did seem to matter anymore, as James thought about it, but he still couldn't help but wonder how all of this destruction could have come about in such a short amount of time. "So, were you clear down at the border when the - the sickness hit?" he asked.

Dave didn't answer right away, he seemed to be thinking pretty hard. "I guess I don't really know when the sickness first hit. Thinking back on it, I'm not sure anyone knows. Six days ago, our unit was ordered away from the border. Our new mission was to set up a quarantine station on I-25 at Castle Rock. They outfitted us in hazmat suits that we were supposed to wear full time, and we were to stop everyone and anyone coming north. Anyone coming from the south was to be placed in quarantine. They had special doctors set up to check everybody out. None of us knew what the doctors were looking for. Not until people started dying, that is." He trailed off, deep in thought again. "Once the first refugees started getting sick and dying, we didn't mind the hazmat suits anymore. But then, soldiers started getting sick, too. Soldiers that had been sealed in those suits just started getting sick and dying, just like the refugees. Jesus, even the doctors started getting sick. Guess that's when I first realized how bad it was. When the doctors and nurses started dying right along with everyone else."

"Did they say what it was? What it is?" James still just could not understand.

"No one ever said. At least, no one ever said for sure. They just called it V1. Thinking back on it, I'm sure none of those doctors or anyone else really knew for sure. At first, the word was that it was some kind of biological, like maybe germ warfare or something." Dave had a little bit of an incongruous grin as he continued. "People started talking about that old Stephen King story, *The Stand*. Don't know if you've read it or not, but I heard one of the guys say we were probably going to be okay as long as we didn't hear the sound of Randall Flagg's boots." Dave actually chuckled a little at that memory. "Anyway, Captain Rogers put that theory to bed. He told us that it was definitely not germ warfare. He said it was some kind of new virus or something. The thing that didn't make any sense to me, was how a virus, any virus, could spread fast enough to kill everyone in just a few days."

That was the very question that kept playing through James' mind, over and over. "Yeah," he said. "It just doesn't make any sense, does it? How the hell could it hit everyone all at once?"

"I did get a chance to ask Doctor Welch that very question," Dave continued. "You know what he told me? He said they figured it didn't infect everyone all at once, it just seemed that way. He said the CDC was working on the assumption that the virus had been infecting people for quite a while and then just lying dormant. Just being carried around like herpes or something, with no symptoms at all until something triggered it. He said that's what they were really trying to figure out. What triggered the virus, and how it happened to everyone all at nearly the same time. Guess if they could have figured it out, they'd also know why it didn't trigger in people like us."

James thought about it. *What if it was just delayed in some people? What if it was still going to strike them all dead, just like the rest, but triggered at a different time.* Even as he felt the fear of the possibility, he felt that he knew that wasn't the case. He somehow instinctively knew or thought he knew, that people like him and Don, and Dave, and his mother, were somehow immune from V-1, whatever it was.

"Anyway," Dave was still talking, "I don't think they ever figured it out. Kind of funny isn't it. Killed them all before they ever figured out what it was that was doing the killing. Course it might not have got them all. Might be someone still trying to figure it out somewhere, but they sure as hell aren't in Castle Rock, Colorado."

Chapter 14

It had been almost two months since the great dying, as James had come to think of that week in May when the world had ended. Or, at least the world that anyone had ever known had ended. It was early in the morning and the temperature on the patio thermometer hadn't yet hit a hundred. With a slight breeze, and shaded from the early morning sun, it was comfortable enough that James and Dave were finishing up their breakfast on the patio. They were eating bacon and eggs; the last of the eggs, as a matter of fact. They probably wouldn't be finding any more, not unless they ventured out into the country somewhere to find some chickens. The eggs they were eating this morning had been liberated from a Whole Foods refrigerated warehouse right after the great dying. There may have still been eggs in that warehouse, but they would surely be totally rotten by now. The power grid, communications networks, and pretty much all of modern infrastructure had died along with the people who operated and maintained it. James wondered how many self-sufficient places like the Mendez estate were still functional. They still had electric power and most of the conveniences that went with it. They were definitely better off than most of the other survivors they'd seen on their foraging runs into what was left of the city. There seemed to be more survivors than James had originally thought there were. He and Dave had discussed it quite a bit and their best guess was that the great death had probably killed somewhere around ninety-nine percent of people on the eastern slope. If that guess was close, somewhere between thirty-five and forty thousand people would have survived in the Denver greater metro area. They had no way of knowing about the rest of the world, but, since there was no evidence to the contrary, they had decided that the survival rate was most likely about the same worldwide.

Surviving the great death was actually the easy part. That was simply the luck of the cosmic draw. The great death, or V-1, or whatever you wanted to call it, had killed most people while sparing just a few lucky survivors. How lucky it was to be a survivor was somewhat questionable. Continued survival after the great death wasn't very easy for people who had only known the structure and convenience of modern civilization.

"We need to get more water today," James broke the silence of the morning. The electricity on the Mendez estate might still be flowing, but the water was not. The taps had run dry less than a week after James and Noni had brought Dave back to the estate. No one knew if there was a broken main, or if the treatment plant had shut down, or what caused the city water to stop flowing. Hell, James didn't even know where the water came from. It had just always been there when he turned on the tap. Not anymore, though.

"Think we can find any closer, or do you plan on going back out to that water train in Commerce City?" Dave asked, referring to a whole train of water tankers they'd found stalled on the tracks.

"Guess it wouldn't hurt to look, but we probably better just do our looking on the way up to Commerce

City, don't you think?" James was worried about conserving diesel in the old water truck that Dave had got rigged up to haul water. Dave had been a real godsend that way. Where James was not that mechanically inclined, Dave seemed to be able to make just about anything work.

When the water pipes went dry, James had been ready to panic, but Dave had simply said, "let's go find some water". And they did. First, they found an old antique Western Star ten-wheeler with a water tank that still had the words, *Potable Water*, printed on the side. The old truck was parked out in the back lot of an Aurora City shop. There hadn't been anyone at all anywhere around the shop, so Dave and James had just broken into the yard and then into the shop. Not only did they find the truck, but they also found all of the hoses and tools that Dave said they'd need. The old truck wouldn't start, of course, but Dave found an old battery charger in the shop that would work off of the Rivian's 110-volt outlet. The fuel tanks on the old water truck were nearly full and the diesel hadn't gone bad, which meant that the City of Aurora had been using the truck fairly recently. James couldn't imagine why they would have been using it at all. Not with all of the electric trucks at their disposal, but he was sure glad that they had. Not only did Dave know how to get the old truck going, he knew how to drive it. James wouldn't have had a clue. It had also been Dave's idea to look for one of the water trains that had been used to transport water from the Great Lakes. All in all, James and Noni probably wouldn't have known how to survive without Dave's help; or at least they wouldn't have been surviving in such relative comfort.

The morning breeze shifted from the southwest to the north and brought with it the stench of death from Denver. The smell of rotting human corpses was always in the background, but sometimes, when the wind was right, it was almost overpowering. That was the worst part of going into the city whenever they had to get water or more food from the abandoned stores and warehouses. James thought about how much food there was available; enough canned goods and non-perishables to last a lifetime, especially if you wanted to eat Allpro. There were warehouses full of the stuff. What had been stored to feed many millions of people for a week or two, was enough to feed the few thousands of survivors for a very long time. That was especially true since the survivors seemed to be abandoning the city. The number of people that James and Dave saw on their outings had steadily diminished over the past couple of months. They had seen people leaving the city going every direction over that time span. Some traveling alone, and some small groups of two to six people traveling together. They had stopped and talked to many of the people they ran into on their "shopping" trips. It was interesting to James that everyone seemed eager to talk and no one seemed the least bit interested in stealing from anyone else anymore. He wasn't sure if that was simply because almost anything anyone could want was available for the taking, or if it had to do with the fact that there were so few people left anymore that hurting anyone else who had survived was simply unthinkable. Though most of those leaving the city were leaving on foot, Dave and James had both been surprised to come across a few others in vehicles of various sorts as well.

Dave finished the cup of instant coffee he'd been nursing and turned his gaze from the mountains toward James. "You know James, I've been thinking about leaving." He said it thoughtfully, not stating that he was leaving, but putting the thought out there to start a conversation.

"Why?" James obviously found the thought a little absurd. *Why would anyone want to leave, when they had everything they needed right here?* At least they had enough to survive, that is.

"I don't know," Dave continued, "Guess it seems like I can't just stay holed up here forever. The great death might have missed me, but death is still going to find me sometime." He paused, thinking about it, then added; "You know, I'm not a religious man, but something keeps coming back to me from the bible. That part about going forth to multiply and replenish the earth." He chuckled under his breath. "Maybe I'm just horny, but I think I need to go forth and do my part."

James laughed out loud. *Dave was horny. How could any twenty-one or twenty-two-year-old man not be?* He had to admit he was horny himself, but not just horny; he was finding himself dreaming and thinking about Anna more and more. *Did she survive? If so, where is she now?* He'd been thinking more and more about leaving, also; maybe talking his mother into heading out to Kremmling. He thought about Noni now. He wasn't at all sure that she would be willing to go anywhere. She didn't do much of anything anymore

~ 215 ~

but sit and stare into space. Whole days would go by that she hardly even got out of bed. James was worried that she was going to simply sit there and waste away.

"Maybe we can find some women in town to bring back here," he said, more to get his mind off Anna and keep the conversation going than anything else.

"Maybe…" Dave mused. "But there's more to it than that. I think I want to head north. Maybe Montana, or even up to Canada; get away from the heat…the heat and the smell," he added as another blast from the city hit the two of them.

"Damn, you'd think it would go away, wouldn't you?" James got up as he spoke. It was too hot and too smelly to sit on the patio anymore. The air conditioning inside the house not only kept the heat at bay, but it also held the stench down to a minimum as well. "Let's go get some water. If you're really thinking about leaving, maybe you better teach me to drive that thing," he said half-jokingly, referring to the old water truck.

James didn't think that Dave would really leave, or maybe he just couldn't imagine not having Dave around, but he figured it would be a good idea to learn to drive that old water truck, anyway. He'd never be able to learn to do everything that Dave had done to make the estate as livable as it was, but he could certainly learn to drive an old diesel truck. He was thinking about how handy and mechanically able Dave was, as they disconnected the hose from the water truck that Dave had rigged up to supply water to the house using gravity. With the truck parked on top of the landscape mound in the middle of the circle drive, the hose that was connected to the outside faucet supplied actual running water to the house. With so little head pressure, it may have only been a trickle, but it was running water, nonetheless.

Driving the old Western Star wasn't as hard as James had thought it would be. It had power steering and an automatic transmission, which Dave had said was rare in a truck this old. The hard part to get used to was the physical size of the thing; learning where the right side of the vehicle was on the road seemed especially trying. It didn't help that you couldn't simply drive down a road or a street to get where you wanted to go. Getting anywhere required working your way around stalled vehicles, all kinds of trash and debris, and the occasional dead body rotting in the sun. It was a slow trip getting anywhere, let alone clear over to the train in Commerce City. With James learning to drive, and Dave following in the Rivian, they didn't get to the train until midday.

The air conditioning didn't work in the old Western Star, and James felt like he was sitting in a pool of sweat by the time they got there. He steered the old truck toward the spot where they'd got their last load of water a few weeks ago. It was a low point alongside the railroad tracks, where the rails were built on a raised embankment crossing over an old natural drainage. The drainage didn't look right, as James eased the truck down the slope to get low enough to use gravity to fill the truck from the tank cars above. He didn't remember the drainage channel having any sign that water had actually run down it at any time in the near past. Now, it looked like a significant stream had run through the box culvert under the train at some point. It wasn't that it was wet, it was dry as a bone, but James had to stop to keep from driving into a channel that was about a foot deep. It looked like the channel had been formed by too much water rushing through the drainage, headed downstream toward the South Platte River.

James punched the yellow diamond-shaped button on the dash and heard the reassuring sound of the air release that set the truck's brakes. It was only after he climbed out of the cab that he saw what had caused a big enough flow of water to cut a channel in the old drainage bottom. Below the center of every one of the water tank cars, sitting on the rails above, the railroad embankment had a ditch cut in the bank, where the valves had been opened and the precious water had flowed down into the drainage. At first, he couldn't quite believe he was seeing what he thought he was. He scrambled up the rail embankment, Dave, who had parked the Rivian right behind him, was already at the top of the bank looking at the open valves on the nearest car.

"Son of a bitch!" Dave exclaimed. "What the…" he trailed off, as he looked up and down the tracks at the other water tankers that had also been emptied.

"How… who?" James stammered, as he reached the top of the embankment and realized that the water was gone. "Who would do something like this?"

"Jesus! Fuck!" Dave was not at a loss for words. "It's fucking insane! This is just fucking insane." His voice calmed a little as the scope of what he was seeing hit home. "It is insane. It had to have been a crazy person. No one in their right mind would have drained these tanks."

Dave's right, of course, James thought. *No one in their right mind would have wasted all of that water*. It hadn't dawned on him until then that some of those who survived the great death might be insane, or evil, or both. Of course, simply being a survivor caused some insanity. It seemed to James that his mother was proof of that. Noni may have been wasting away out of grief, but she wasn't evil. This; this wasting of water for no apparent reason was purely evil. *What kind of person would do such a thing? How could someone that survived the great death even think about wasting the water that was needed to survive?*

Dave walked down the line of cars, checking each one as he went. James just stood there watching, knowing that whoever had done this hadn't done it half-assed. He knew Dave wouldn't find any water left in any of the tank cars. He made his way back down the slope, thinking about what they should do now; wondering if they could find another source of water where they'd be able to fill their tank. Thinking about what they should do, if they couldn't. Thinking about how fucking hot it was. The temperature had to be over a hundred and ten degrees. He climbed into the air-conditioned comfort of the Rivian to wait for Dave to come back.

"What now?" Dave asked as he took his place in the passenger seat. He'd only checked about a dozen cars before deciding it was no use.

James had been trying to decide *what now?* ever since he crawled into the Rivian. "Damn, I don't know," he answered. "I'm kind of wondering if you might be right about leaving. Even if we can find another source of water, how do we know it'll be there next time?" He had a thought, even as he asked the question. The South Platte was just about a quarter of a mile away over on the other side of the tracks. He put the Riv in reverse and backed out of the drainage. They'd have to go down the tracks a little to find a place to cross, but James decided that they needed to see if there was water in the river. Maybe they could find some kind of pump and a place where they could pump water straight out of the river into the water truck. Dave could probably figure out how to do it.

Seeing the mostly dry riverbed was probably even more of a disappointment than finding all of the water gone from the train had been. Knowing that they'd been in an extreme drought for at least the past decade didn't make looking at the dried-up river any easier. The riverbed wasn't completely dry. There were a few small puddles where whatever small amount of water that was still trickling through the gravelly bottom pooled on the surface.

"Maybe we could dig enough of a hole to pump water from," Dave said, apparently picking up on James' thoughts. "Take a pretty good hole, though. Wonder if we can find a backhoe or something to dig with?"

James shrugged. He wasn't feeling exactly optimistic about anything. Dave could probably find a backhoe and a pump, and rig the whole thing up to get water, but James knew that he couldn't. It struck him that he and Noni had only been able to go on living at home the way they had because of Dave. It wasn't a good feeling; the realization that the easy life he'd been handed on a golden platter had left him so ill-prepared for the world they now inhabited. He took a deep breath, exhaled and said, "You're right about leaving Dave. We should get out of here. Get away to the country somewhere." He looked around. "This is nothing but a dead city. The great death killed a lot more than just people, didn't it?"

There was still a couple of hundred gallons of water left in the four-thousand-gallon tank, so James parked the water truck back in its place on top of the berm, and he and Dave reconnected the hoses to enable the use of that remaining water. It was late in the evening by then and the sun was just starting to drop behind the mountains to the west. With the sky totally dry and devoid of clouds, it would be another in a long line of bland, unremarkable sunsets. For some reason, James was thinking about how sunsets had seemed a lot prettier when he was young.

Dave had taken the Riv to the car barn to charge it back up, and James expected to find Noni sitting in her favorite chair in the living room. He had made up his mind, and he wanted to tell her his plan right away. His plan was to take her and enough supplies to get them there, and to make the journey to Kremmling. He hoped they would find Grandpa Chuck alive and well; and, truth be told, he wanted nothing more than to find Anna. Maybe they could talk Dave into going with them, maybe not. It didn't really matter anymore. What really mattered was getting away from the dead city, and James and Dave must not have been the only ones who thought so. Today's outing had been the first time that they had failed to see another living human being. Everyone, it seemed, had already deserted the death and the rot;

all that was left of the once thriving Denver Metro area.

"Mom," he yelled when he didn't find her in the living room. No answer. He looked in the kitchen, no one there. "Hey Mom, we're home" he yelled a little louder, heading toward her bedroom. He thought he heard a moan coming through the open door, and hurried into her room.

Noni was there, in her king size bed. Her face was as white as the sheet that was pulled up to her chin. As white as that part of the sheet, that is. Much of the sheet wasn't white at all. It was dark red and wet; soaked in blood. Noni was lying in a pool of blood. She was moaning in pain and there was a fear in her eyes that James would never forget.

He rushed to the side of the bed and fell to his knees. "Mother…mother," he didn't know what to say. His mother was obviously dying. *Why?*

"Don't cry son," her voice was weak. James hadn't even realized he was crying at all. "It's the cancer. I'm sorry James, I should have told you. Ovarian cancer. Same as killed Mom…was supposed to have a hysterectomy, but then…but then Dr. Yew…gone. All gone. So sorry, James. So sorry."

"It's okay, Mom. It's all okay." James was on the verge of sobbing.

"No!" her voice was suddenly much more forceful than seemed possible. "It's not okay. Shouldn't have let him…" the words were getting softer, trailing off. "Shouldn't have let your father keep you from Anna…oh James…I'm so sorry…so, so sorry." She gasped in a sudden intake of air and then lay still, her eyes opened wide but now devoid of life.

Early the following morning, Dave helped bury Noni out in the flower garden turned cemetery. "I'm leaving," he told James after the last shovel full of dirt was placed on the grave.

"I know," James said flatly. He was totally drained of emotion and exhaustion was weighing him down. He hadn't slept at all in more than twenty-four hours, and his thoughts were random and scattered. "You should take the Riv," he told Dave.

"What will you do? Now, I mean. Now that your mother's gone. You should come with me."

"No," James answered slowly. "No, I'm not sure what I'm going to do now. Maybe go to Kremmling…should have taken her to Kremmling." He gestured toward his mother's fresh grave with his chin.

James had talked enough about the BR Ranch and Kremmling that Dave knew what he meant. He also knew that James hoped to have loved ones still alive out there. James had broached the subject of all of them going to Kremmling a couple of times, but Dave had always shrugged it off. He hadn't told James how hard it was to be there with two people who still had each other when everyone he had ever loved was gone. He hadn't ever told him how much harder he thought it would be to live among even more family members. He didn't want to live with a loving family that he could never be a part of. No, Dave had made up his mind that he would go north. Somewhere, someday, he would find his own love. It was time to start his own family; a new family, a new life, in a strange new world.

James woke suddenly. It took him a moment or two before he realized where he was. He was stretched out in his recliner with a light blanket covering him. He pushed the button, the recliner raised him to an upright sitting position. Memory streamed into his consciousness, leaving him, once again, empty and alone. He remembered sitting down in the recliner after he and Dave had finished burying Noni. He remembered sitting there and thinking. It was fairly early in the day when he'd sat down. It was now dark. The house was totally dark, with the light of the moon through the big picture window casting an eerie glow on his surroundings. He didn't know how long he'd been asleep, but it must have been near midnight, judging by how high in the sky the moon seemed to be. Dave must have covered me, he thought, remembering that he didn't have a blanket when he'd sat down. He pushed the blanket off and stood up. Walking as quietly as he could, so as not to awaken him, he went down the hall to Dave's room. The door was open, and the moonlight fell on an empty bed in an empty room. He'd done it, then; Dave was gone. With no need to be quiet anymore, James strode back to the kitchen. He was hungry. It didn't seem right to want to eat, but his body seemed to be on autopilot, as he opened a can of Allpro and started filling the emptiness in his stomach. That, at least, was one emptiness that could be filled.

Chapter 15

James was carrying his third cup of instant coffee, sipping it as he walked out to the car barn. The Rivian was gone. *Good for him,* he thought. He was glad that Dave had taken the Riv. Where James was headed it probably wouldn't have been much use, anyway. He'd given it a lot of thought and based on how badly clogged the streets and roads were in Denver, he didn't think there was much chance that any of the roads leading over the mountains would be passable by car. If Dave headed north and stayed out in the plains, he could probably take the Riv off-road to get around the stalled vehicles that would inevitably block the way. That was most probably not the case for one who was headed west over the mountains. Every route over the mountains that James could think of had stretches of road along rivers and through canyons where there were drop-offs on one side and cliffs or steep mountains on the other. Just a couple of stalled autonomous trucks or cars would render those stretches of road impassable by car or truck. No, he wouldn't take any of the cars or trucks in the warehouse, he would ride to Kremmling on his old motorcycle.

James hadn't been on the old Zero for at least five years, so he needed to get it charged up and ready to go. He plugged it in and checked the tires, glad to find that they still held air. They were low on pressure, so he started the air compressor, found a tire gauge and aired them up. While he was getting the bike ready, he was remembering how angry his mother had been, when his dad had allowed him to have a dirt bike on his fourteenth birthday. She'd ranted and raved for a full day about how dangerous motorcycles were. She'd been right, of course. He had to smile at the memory of how much angrier she had become when he crashed for the first time. Fortunately, he had never been seriously injured, just a few scrapes and bruises, but no broken bones.

Thinking about Noni was mostly what he'd been doing, so the memory of her fear of motorcycles was just one more thread in the tapestry of the memories of his mother. He wished that he had taken her to Kremmling as soon as they'd buried Julie. She had deserved to see the BR Ranch again before she died, whether or not Grandpa Chuck was still alive. James had a feeling that Chuck was alive. He also had the same feeling regarding Anna, only stronger. He imagined what that reunion would have been like. Riding the Zero up the ranch lane from Highway 9, with his mother on the back. The mental image made him laugh out loud, in spite of his grief. There was no way in hell that he could have ever talked Noni into riding to Kremmling on the back of a motorcycle.

The backpack seemed too heavy, but James was sure it would be alright. He'd already pared it down to what he thought he might need. He would just have to get used to it. He wasn't even packing his own water. He had figured out a way to tie two jugs of water onto the sides of the bike. That should be plenty to get him up into the mountains, where he was sure he'd be able to get all the water he needed. He had the same water purification filter in his pack that he'd carried from Colorado College. The gate was still closed, Dave had gone to the trouble of locking it up and climbing over when he left. *Probably no need for that now*, James thought, as he went in the gatehouse and opened the gate for the last time. He'd left the power on and the air conditioner running, just like he intended to return. Maybe someone would find it like that, maybe not. Eventually, the systems would all break down or malfunction and the Mendez Estate would be as dead as the people buried in the flower garden behind the house. He pulled through the ornate open gate, stopped and turned for one last look, before pulling out of the drive onto the roadway, headed for an unknown future at the Blue River Ranch.

Even though he coasted all the way down the west side of Loveland Pass, the Zero ran out of juice just about a mile west of the old Keystone Resort. James hadn't planned on being able to get all the way to the BR on the bike, it was simply too far for the Zero's range. He had thought it would be close, but there were just too many stalled vehicles abandoned all along I-70. Working his way around, between, and through the dead cars and trucks had drained the Zero's battery pack faster than he'd anticipated. Plus, he'd decided to not even try to get through the tunnel, and the route over Loveland Pass added, not just extra miles, but extra uphill miles.

The old Keystone Ski Resort had been mostly abandoned years before the great death. Like all ski resorts in Colorado, it had been the victim of multiple factors. Not the least of which was the end of heavy winter snowpack and the overall lack of water for making snow. That, and the lack of skiers, as the world's economies had all nose-dived over the past decade or so. James had fond memories of snowboarding down the slopes that were still the dominant feature of Keystone Mountain. The lifts were still there, hanging above the green open slopes surrounded by what was left of the forest; as many brown dead trees as green. *It's kind of a minor miracle*, he thought, *that the whole place hasn't already burned. Probably won't be much longer before a lightning bolt from a dry mountain thunderstorm hits the right tree and ignites a firestorm that will take it all out, just like the other side of Loveland Pass.* It seemed like he'd already seen more burned forest than live trees. Even the living forests were, like this one, more than half dead already.

James dropped the Zero on its side at the edge of old Highway 6. He left the water jugs, along with the bike, and started off toward Dillon on foot. From now on, hiking on foot, he would only be able to carry what water he had in the bladder in his backpack. That would do. It wasn't that much farther to the Blue River Ranch. The mountain streams and rivers didn't flow like they used to, but he was sure that he would be able to find enough pools and trickles to keep the bladder supplied with filtered water. He stopped and looked back at the dirt bike laying on the ground at the side of the road. It was the last of it, the last of his old life. He turned and started walking briskly west, the backpack and the old .300 Weatherby that was slung over his shoulder seeming to get heavier as he thought about all the miles that lay ahead.

The sun was about to go down by the time James got through what remained of Dillon and Silverthorne. He remembered hearing about the wildfire that had burned through most of the area, including the twin communities, back in 2030. There wasn't much that had been rebuilt after that. There was no need. The tourism and ski traffic that had caused the towns to boom in the last half of the twentieth century was gone forever. He was pretty well exhausted, and he knew that he probably hadn't even covered ten miles yet. He hadn't seen another living person since Georgetown, and those two people he only saw from a distance. They had appeared to be working a garden on the outskirts of town, over across the valley from the interstate. There was plenty of wildlife. The great death virus or whatever it was didn't seem to affect any animals other than humans. Of course, there was no way he could know that for sure. For all he knew, it might have wiped out all primates, or pigs for that matter, but he didn't see any indication that it had been at all harmful to the fauna that was native to the Rocky Mountains.

He had been pleasantly surprised to find that there was still some water in Dillon Reservoir; not much, but there was a stream of water still flowing on down the Blue River. That was a really good sign. If there was water flowing down the Blue here, there would still be water at the BR. James was feeling pretty exhausted, though he knew he'd only walked ten or twelve miles. As much as he wanted to get there, he knew he couldn't just keep walking all night. It had to be at least another twenty miles to the ranch. Maybe, with a good night's rest, he would be able to do the rest tomorrow. As he walked, watching for a good place to camp for the night, he saw a wisp of smoke rising from behind a clump of trees on the other side of a small hill. At first, he feared it might be a wildfire, it was just beyond the line that marked the boundary between what had been destroyed by the big fire of 2030 and the forest that had been spared. James marveled at the mysterious way some forest had been spared and some had been utterly incinerated. As he followed Highway 9 on around the hill and got close enough, he decided it had to be a cooking fire. There was the unmistakable smell of some kind of roasting meat in the air.

Once he got around the small hill, some very old ranch buildings came into view. The ranch had to have been there long before there was ever a Dillon Reservoir or a Keystone Ski Resort; long before there was ever an interstate highway running through Silverthorne. Just to look at it, James would have guessed it to be as old as the Blue River Ranch. It was probably homesteaded at about the same time as his great-great-great-grandfather had settled the Blue River Ranch, twenty miles or so down the valley. *Had to have been some hardy people that staked out this area,* he thought. *This might have been the BR's closest neighbors back then.* Back in the 1800s, this high up, the winters would have been terrible. James had skied both Keystone and Breckenridge as a youngster and had learned enough history from visiting the local museums to know how much different the area's climate had once been. It was hard to believe how much the climate had changed in just the past fifteen years, let alone the past hundred and fifty. James was contemplating those changes as he walked up the short lane to the ranch house.

The cooking fire was on the backside of the house, so James walked on toward the old barn instead of walking up to the door. On the backside of the house, in an open area of bare ground, there was a man turning something on a spit that had been improvised over a rock-lined fire pit. James couldn't tell what the animal was, but it smelled delicious.

"Hello," he called out, trying not to startle the man too badly.

The man did kind of jump, obviously startled more than James had intended, but he seemed friendly enough when he turned toward James and said, "Howdy do. Sure wasn't expecting anybody walking up on me like that." He turned back to the house and hollered, "Hey Jack, Rita, we've got company."

A young blonde woman came out of the old-fashioned wooden screen door, followed by another dark-haired man. The woman was about James' age; the man probably eight or ten years older than James. Both seemed as happy to see another living person as James was to see them.

"Come on in," the man who had been tending the barbecue said. He walked out toward James. They met at the edge of the dried-up lawn. "Jack Thompson," the man said, extending his hand to James. "And that's my brother Ray, and Rita McKendrick," he added, as they shook hands.

James introduced himself and shook hands with Rita, who had followed closely behind Jack, and then he walked over to shake Ray's hand and see what was cooking. Ray had taken over the cooking spot at the fire, vacated by his brother Jack. At first, James couldn't tell for sure what was cooking; his first guess was that it was a small deer, maybe this year's fawn, but it seemed too fat and stubby. Ray informed him that it was lamb. He said there were quite a few sheep roaming around the mountains, but he didn't know for how long. "Figured we better salvage some while we can," Ray told him. "Before the bears and lions get 'em all." He went on to tell James how they had gathered a small flock that they had grazing somewhere off a ways to the west. "Connie's watch tonight," he added, explaining that there were actually four of them living on this old ranch, but someone had to tend to the flock.

It turned out that Connie was Rita's sister, and it didn't take long for James to realize that these two surviving brothers had somehow found two surviving sisters, and the four of them were starting over together here on this old abandoned ranch.

"So, what brings you here to our humble abode?" Ray asked. "We haven't seen many people since – since…" he didn't have to finish the sentence.

"Since the great dying," James finished it for him. "That's what I call it, anyway."

"Yeah, the great dying. Guess that's as good as any. What the hell was it, anyway? We've been trying to figure it out ever since everyone died."

James told them what he knew, which wasn't much, but at least they were a little relieved to hear that it wasn't some kind of biological, or germ warfare.

"Were you guys living here before?" James asked, even though he was pretty sure that was not the case.

Jack answered. "Oh no, Ray and I are both from Glenwood. We just had to leave after – after most everyone died. It's a terrible thing to lose your family. How 'bout you, where are you from?"

James was relieved for some reason that none of the three had apparently connected him to Robert Mendez. Of course, why would they, Mendez was a fairly common name. He decided to keep it that way, no reason for them to know his true past. Nothing from his previous life seemed to matter anymore; maybe that was best. "I'm from Denver," he told them, "headed for my Grandpa's ranch down by Kremmling. Guess I had to get out of Denver, same as you having to get out of Glenwood. Just wasn't anything to stay for." He went on to tell them how it seemed like most everyone that survived had already left the rotting city.

They wanted to know if he'd walked all the way from Denver; why they hadn't seen more people from the city up this way, and on and on. He told them it seemed to him like most of those who had survived had headed north; that he would have headed north, too, except for the chance that he hoped to find family still alive on the BR Ranch.

Jack, Ray, and Rita were all sympathetic and told him that they hoped he would find his Grandpa alive, but James could tell they didn't really think he would. They invited him to join them for an evening meal and even invited him to spend the night in the hayloft of the old barn instead of trying to find a place to camp. How could he refuse? Other than Dave and his mother, James had hardly talked to another person in more than two months. It was good to listen to other people's stories, even if the stories just confirmed that the great death had probably hit everywhere, not just on the eastern slope of Colorado.

Jack and Ray had grown up in Glenwood and were both still living there when it hit. James had the feeling, as he listened to their life story, that they had come from a locally powerful family. He couldn't recall ever hearing anything about the Thompson's of Glenwood Springs, so they must not have been in the same class as Robert Mendez, but then, who was?

The Thompson brothers had apparently been the owners of several car dealerships on the western slope. The family business their father had started had done well enough that they were pretty well off, even after most people could no longer afford to buy cars. Ray and Jack had both been married and lost their wives to the great death. Jack had also lost a two-year-old son. His younger brother Ray didn't have children. Like James, the pain of their loss was still really strong. He wondered how much the passage of time would be able to ease pain like that.

Rita was crying by the time Jack finished telling James about losing his wife and two-year-old son. Ray put his arm around her and held her, as he asked James, "What about you? How did Robert Mendez' son end up out here with us lesser folk?"

So much for anonymity. "Didn't think you knew," James said.

"I didn't know for sure, just a hunch. Mendez Investments handled a lot of our family's money over the years. I never met Robert personally, but I thought I remembered him having a son named James. I take it the great death, as you call it, didn't spare the ultra-wealthy, either."

"No," James began, "it didn't spare anybody. Just us. I mean just the few of us, like you guys, who were immune - somehow. How, or why we didn't die too, I guess we'll never know. Kind of makes you feel guilty, doesn't it? Living, while everyone else dies." He went on to tell them his whole story, from that day back in May when he and Julie had fled Colorado College, right up to the present. When he got to the part about the death of his mother, Rita went from weeping to outright sobbing.

"We had to bury our mother, too," she got out between sobs. By then there were no dry eyes left at the table. There was a catharsis in sharing each other's stories of death and grief, and the men prodded and encouraged Rita to open up and let it out. She told them about her and her sister, Connie, growing up on a sheep ranch outside Montrose. She was twenty-two and Connie was a year younger. Their father had died of a heart attack four years ago. The two of them had been helping their mother run the ranch when *it* hit. They'd buried their mother in the yard, just like James had done, but they hadn't left immediately. At first, they'd thought they would just keep on living as they had. Neither of them had ever known anything different. They'd lived on the ranch outside Montrose their entire lives. Both had lost boyfriends that lived in town. Rita had actually gotten engaged just a couple of weeks before it happened.

"You know, IT was just the final blow," she said. "We didn't leave her any choice."

The men exchanged some questioning glances. "Who?" James asked. "Who didn't you leave any choice?"

Rita gave him a look that said he should know exactly what she was talking about. "We!' she said emphatically. "We – the human race. We didn't leave her any other choice. Mother Nature. Don't you see? Mother Nature – Mother Earth; call her God if you want to. Whatever you want to call her, IT was the only option left. We declared war on nature long ago." Rita had gone from a grieving young woman to a priestess delivering a sermon. "The Anthropocene they called it. Call it what you want, it was a war against nature. And you know the funny part? The funny part is we killed ourselves. Somehow, it was forgotten that we are also nature. If you look at Mother Earth and everything she contains as a living entity, mankind was like a cancer. IT, the great death, as you call it," she said, looking at James, "was just an immune response. Nothing more than a cure for a disease."

All three men stared at Rita silently. James could tell that Ray and Jack were as stunned as he was. Rita, having delivered her sermon, looked right back at them, like she was waiting for a rebuttal. None was forthcoming. He didn't know what the other two were thinking, but James thought Rita made a good argument. Problem was, he didn't believe in God; did that mean he didn't believe in nature? How can you not believe in nature? It's everywhere. It's all around us. And then the thought hit him, *it is us. We are nature. She's right about that, for sure*.

James needed to change the subject. "How did you guys all meet up?" he asked, to no one in particular.

Jack was as ready for a change of subject as James was. "I guess Connie and Rita just kind of saved us."

He smiled at the memory. "Ray and I decided we couldn't stay in Glenwood. It was mainly the smell that got us. Living in Glenwood, you get used to the smell of the sulfur water, but I don't think you can ever get used to the smell of so many dead people. There were way too many dead for us and the others that survived to bury or deal with at all. Some of the others left before we did. They headed out different directions…wonder where they ended up? Anyway, after about a month of no comms, and nobody coming to the rescue, we decided that Glenwood must not have been the only place hit by IT. So, we decided to head east, thinking maybe IT might not have hit as hard on the eastern slope. We thought maybe some of the big hospitals might have been able to save more than survived in Glenwood…you know, we used to have a pretty good medical system in Glenwood." Jack looked into the distance, his mind obviously off on a tangent.

"We figured the canyon would be totally blocked," Ray picked up where Jack had left off. "So, we put on our backpacks; Jack and I have always been avid hikers. Anyway, we just started hiking toward Denver. We were just about to Vail when Connie and Rita rode up behind us. Their dogs like to scared us to death."

"Not exactly what Connie and I expected to find, when we left Montrose," Rita actually laughed, obviously back from her pseudo-religious rant. "Of course, we didn't really know what we were going to find. We just knew the sheep ranch wasn't going to cut it anymore." She laughed again. "And here we are raising sheep again. But at least we've got help," she added, putting her arm affectionately around Ray.

It was obvious that these two brothers and two sisters had, for want of a better term, mated up. James wondered about human nature. In the face of the death of so many people, instinct drove men and women together. The sex drive was a powerful instinct. Maybe the most powerful of all. These two couples had come together, not through love, but through the instinctual desire to mate, to procreate, to ensure that the human race would continue. They might come to think of it as love if they hadn't already, but love was just an emotion, probably just a tool used by an age-old instinct.

James was roused out of reflection by Jack rejoining the conversation. "Yeah, don't know where me and Ray would be now if Rita and Connie hadn't come along. Probably not raising sheep in the middle of nowhere." It was Jack's turn to laugh now. "Course I guess every where's the middle of nowhere anymore."

Eventually, James heard the whole story. Connie and Rita had set out from Montrose on horseback hoping to find somewhere, anywhere that hadn't been devastated by IT. James still preferred *the great death*, but IT was the only way the others referred to the virus or whatever it was. They'd ridden to Grand Junction first, but had headed toward I-70 through Palisade after the smell on Orchard Mesa turned them around. By the time they caught up to Jack and Ray, after passing through Rifle, Glenwood, and the lesser towns along the way, their only hope was that the devastation was contained to the western slope. In truth, they'd given up hope. If there was any functioning government left in Denver, some kind of help would have already arrived.

When they came upon Jack and Ray, the four of them had seemed to come to a nearly instantaneous mutual decision to go on together. They'd ridden doubled up the rest of the way to this old ranch outside Silverthorne. Much like James, the four of them had been looking for a place to camp for the night, when they came upon the ranch buildings. They'd found the corpses of an old man and an old woman in bed together in the master bedroom. Deciding that the old couple deserved a decent burial, they had dug a grave out back and buried them by moonlight, together, in the same grave. It had seemed like that was what the old couple would have wanted. The old house had three bedrooms, and the four had decided that a real bed would feel too good to pass up after several nights on the ground. Nothing was said explicitly about it, but James deduced that they had coupled up that very first night on the ranch. By the next day, they had decided there was no use going any further. Presuming the old couple that they'd buried were the owners, and being sure they wouldn't mind, Ray and Rita, and Jack and Connie had decided to start a new life on the old ranch. It had everything they needed, a well with an antique hand pump for drinking water, the Blue River flowing by for the livestock and a huge garden that had been planted in the spring. The neglected garden had taken quite a bit of work, but Rita said they would get enough vegetables to get them through the next winter. The green salad that they'd served with the lamb had made the shared meal the best James had eaten in months.

The four talked well into the evening before Ray decided it was time for bed. He told James that he was welcome to sleep in the master bedroom, but they'd burned the bed that they found the old couple in. James declined, opting to spend the night in the hayloft of the old barn. A reasonably soft bed of old hay sounded better than a hardwood floor. He also figured there would be a better breeze through the large hayloft doors than there would be through the windows and screen door of the old ranch house.

After a surprisingly good night's sleep, James was still enjoying the cool early morning stillness when he heard the barn doors open below him. The horse in the stall directly beneath where he was laying, neighed a welcome home to the other horse that was being led into the barn. The sun had just come up over the mountains to the east, casting bright streaks of light through the cracks in the sides of the old barn. James quietly watched through the spaces between the boards of the loft floor, as the young woman that had to be Connie, took the saddle off of the palomino she'd brought into the barn, and led him to the stall next to the other palomino. Connie was as blonde as Rita, but she had longer hair flowing down her back from beneath a western style straw hat. James couldn't see her face, but he could see that she was a very well-built young lady. The skimpy shirt and tight jeans gave that away immediately.

James felt a stirring in his pants at the sight of such a sexy young woman and thought about his reaction.

What is it that makes me horny at just the sight of a sexy stranger, he wondered? He ignored the horniness and rolled over to speak down through the hay opening in the loft floor. "You must be Connie," he said.

Connie, startled by the sound of James rolling over, was looking up at him, as he spoke. When she looked up, her face was lit up by a spot of sunshine coming through a knothole in the side of the barn. The effect was that of a spotlight, and she truly was beautiful. She smiled up at him, and said, "I am, and who might you be?"

James introduced himself and told her that he'd already met the others the night before. She crossed over to the ladder into the loft and climbed up. James crawled out of his sleeping bag and pulled on his jeans to cover his obvious sexual interests before her head poked up through the hole in the floor. He was standing shirtless facing her as she turned toward him. Connie looked him up and down; he could actually feel her eyes as they momentarily stopped on the bulge that his jeans could not conceal. Her blue eyes quickly met his, and her face had a definite blush, as she glanced away, and walked over to push some loose hay down through the opening into her horse's manger.

James could do nothing but watch spellbound as she bent over to push the hay. His eyes were fixed on the curves of her butt displayed by the tightness of her jeans. His own jeans felt even more confining by the throbbing they contained. His desire was so irrational that it scared him. *How can I want somebody this much? I don't even know her.*

Connie turned back toward James and walked straight to him. Her face was flushed, not the blush of embarrassment that he thought he'd seen before but flushed with what must have been the same desire he was feeling. Her face was basically fixed, trancelike. She was neither smiling nor frowning. She didn't say a word, as she reached down with both hands and started unbuttoning the jeans he'd just put on. They couldn't get each other's pants off fast enough, as they fell to the sleeping bag. It was over before he knew it.

God, I haven't been that fast since that first time with Maddy, James thought, as he rolled over and quickly started getting dressed.

They got dressed without saying anything to each other at all. James helped her get some hay out of her long blonde hair, as feelings of guilt hit him in waves. He was only a day's hike from Anna. How could he have possibly done what he just did? Anna, who he knew he would always love like no other. Why? Why had he done this thing? And what about Connie? It didn't matter whether or not it had been purely sexual instinct. It didn't matter that he didn't know her at all. In just a matter of minutes, he had developed feelings for her that were as hard to explain as the instant sex they'd just shared.

"I'm sorry," he finally said. "I know you're Jack's woman. I – we had no right."

"I am not Jack's woman," she answered defiantly. "I'm nobody's woman but my own." Then she smiled at him. "Besides, I'd say I'm the one that fucked you, remember."

James hurriedly finished dressing. He had an overwhelming desire to get out of there. He didn't want to face Jack and Connie together. He was afraid of what would be revealed for all to see. "I have to go," he said.

"Go where?" she asked, with a mischievous grin. "Where is there to go? You could just stay here with us."

The thought was horrifying to James. Not that he could say he had no more desire for Connie, but rationality had returned. He was afraid of all that he now knew instinct could compel. He was afraid that if he didn't leave, and leave right now, Jack would probably feel the need to kill him. It was not a comforting thought, but a stark realization that did not bode well at all for all the people who had survived the great death. When civilization dies, the ancient instincts of the caveman return. How would people deal with those instincts? The drive to procreate so strong that a man might be willing to drag a woman by her hair back to his cave to give him babies. Could the rational mind overcome instincts that had been laying mostly dormant for all these thousands of years? It was a question that didn't even need an answer to be terrifying.

Chapter 16

The sun was setting in the west directly in front of James as he walked up the gravel lane from Highway 9 toward the Blue River Ranch Headquarters. He was exhausted. Knowing one could walk twenty miles in a day wasn't the same as actually doing it. His legs ached, and his feet were sore. Every step was one more step too many. When he got to the top of the rise between Highway 9 and the Blue River Ranch, and the ranch buildings finally came into view, the sight didn't give him the lift he'd expected. There was no sign of anyone. The big meadow that stretched away to the north was brown and dying from lack of irrigation. The grasses that should have been knee high were thin and short. There would be no hay crop to cut and gather this year.

To the south of the BR ranch buildings, where it was visible, James could see water flowing in Spider Creek; water that he knew was normally used to irrigate the huge hay meadow. A feeling of dread came over him, as he stopped and took in the apparently lifeless scene. He was almost afraid to go on; afraid of what he was going to find. What if he'd come all this way only to find everyone dead? Steeling himself against the dread, he continued on down the lane toward the big house. He was still a couple of hundred yards from the house when a dog started barking and he finally saw movement. A black and white border collie bounded off of the veranda and started running toward him, but stopped instantly when a man's voice yelled, "Blackie! Stay!"

Chuck Pierson stepped off of the veranda with a rifle in his hand. He carried the old 30-30 carbine loosely in one hand; the barrel pointed at the ground. He walked out to where the dog had stopped in its tracks and continued on toward James. Blackie fell right in step at his heel. James, as tired as his feet and legs were, started running toward his grandfather.

"Well, I'll be…" was about all Chuck could get out at first. James hugged the old man tight without saying anything at all. Blackie stood right behind Chuck, his tail wagging.

"Didn't think I'd ever see you again," Chuck said, with tears in his eyes. "Look at you, all grown up…didn't think I'd see you again," he repeated. "Least not in this life, anyway. Your Mom?"

James didn't have to answer. The look in his eyes told Chuck that his daughter hadn't survived. "Was it the sickness?" Chuck asked.

Crying, James shook his head no, and said, "cancer. She survived the sickness. Cancer killed her. Same as Grandma."

The tears in Chuck's eyes dried up, as he almost imperceptibly shook his head yes. His jaw was set, and he had a faraway look in his eyes. He'd already done his grieving. "Come on son," he said. "You must be exhausted." He turned and started walking back toward the house.

James walked beside him, with Blackie now running ahead of them. Chuck could feel the question, as he noticed James looking around as they walked. "They're all gone," he said, in response to James' unasked question.

James felt like his heart skipped a beat. "Anna?" it was a one-word question.

"Don't know, son," Chuck could feel his grandson's pain. "She was away at school."

James dropped his pack on the floor and leaned his rifle up against the wall before collapsing into the easy chair on the veranda. Chuck went into the house and returned with a large glass of water for each of them. James was hungry, but he had a greater hunger for information than he did for food. The two men spent the next several hours sharing all they knew about loved ones who were no longer there, the great death, and general catch-up. It had been nine years since James and Chuck had sat and shared each other's company on this veranda. To say the world had changed in those intervening years would have been such a gross understatement that neither man even commented on it.

James couldn't help but notice how old his grandfather seemed. Just the toll that age takes on everyone would have been enough, but Chuck had aged far beyond his sixty-eight years of living. His once jet-black hair was now totally white, along with the full beard on his face. James had never known his grandfather to wear a beard, he thought, as he stroked his own. Maybe everybody quit shaving after the great death. Chuck was still lean as ever, maybe more so, and he had the weathered look of one who has spent a good deal of their life doing hard physical work. Other than the white beard, the main features of aging that James noticed were the wrinkles and weakened look of Chuck's neck; and the back of his hands, where the skin seemed thin and stretched despite the wrinkles.

"You really loved her, didn't you?" Chuck said, as James stared at the unfathomable number of stars in the totally dark sky.

"I do love her," James answered, unwilling to put Anna in the past tense. "Where did she go to school?" He had the thought that he might just go wherever it was to find her.

"Oregon, of all places. She followed that worthless Will Donovan to Oregon. They got engaged, you know. What happened James? I know about your secret visit a couple of years ago. I also know you broke her heart. Didn't do much for my feelings either, when you didn't even stop in to say hi."

The pain of ending his relationship with Anna came back to James like it was yesterday. "It was Dad," he said.

"Figured as much," Chuck told him. "Your mother half-assed let me know, but she wouldn't ever openly say anything bad about the son of a bitch. Never understood why she always backed that man, even when she knew it was wrong."

"It was you, Grandpa." James had to tell him. "He would have taken the BR and evicted you. She couldn't let him take this away from you. She didn't have a choice." James paused, the silence between them broken only by the sound of coyotes yipping somewhere off in the distance, and the gentle sound of water running lazily over the rocks of Spider Creek. "You know," he continued, "it took most of my life to learn about my father; to learn what he really was. By the time I knew he was a psychopath, it was too late. Too late for me…for me and Anna."

Chuck didn't say anything for a while. He just took in a deep breath and let it out in a sigh. They sat in silence for several minutes, listening to the soothing sounds of the Colorado night and looking at the milky way stretching across the starlit sky.

Chuck finally spoke. "Don't blame yourself, son," the tone of his voice saying the rest, that there was always plenty of blame to go around. "Besides, maybe Anna's still alive. Just before the comms died, she told Clyde she was headed home. Maybe she'll show up here, same as you. You must be starving," he added, as he got up out of his chair with a groan.

The morning sun shining through the open window brought James back from a deep dreamless sleep. It seemed like he ached all over. His legs hurt so bad that he didn't even want to stretch, let alone get up. It took a little bit to get oriented before he remembered where he was and the conversation with his Grandpa from the night before. He caught the smell of wood smoke drifting up through the open window. Wood smoke and something else; bacon. The smell of frying bacon! He forced his aching legs to carry him over to the open window and looked out. He couldn't see the source of the smoke from this window, the breeze was carrying it around the house from the back. He could see the old house that the Duran's had lived in looking the same as it always had. The huge garden they had always raised didn't look any different than he remembered it, either. In his mind's eye, he could picture the scene as it had been nearly nine years ago; the last time he stood at this window looking out. *Grandpa's been working the garden,* he realized. It wouldn't have looked nearly as good, otherwise. He closed the window and pulled the blinds to block out the morning sun. Better to keep as much of the daytime heat out as possible.

Chuck was bent over the raised fire pit on the patio when James walked out the back door of the house. The old man was frying eggs in a huge cast iron skillet to go with the bacon James had smelled. The fire pit had been turned into a wood grill with the addition of a steel mesh grate over the top. There was an old antique speckled blue enamel coffee pot boiling beside the skillet.

"Still eating bacon and eggs, I see," James greeted his grandfather.

"Not for long, I'm afraid. This is the last of the bacon," Chuck answered. "Grab your cup, coffee's ready."

The patio table had been set for breakfast for two. James grabbed both cups and carried them over for Chuck to fill. The steaming brown liquid had a woody nutty smell that wasn't like any coffee James had ever had before. "What is this?" James asked as he took a sip.

"Chicory," Chuck answered. "Been drinking the stuff for years now. You didn't expect real coffee, did you?"

The chicory beverage had a flavor that was reminiscent of coffee but was definitely not the same. Pretty good, James thought. "Not bad," he told Chuck. "Where'd you get it?"

"Chicory root. It's everywhere. Surprised you've never heard of it." Chuck looked around and pointed to a patch of wild blue weeds growing just past the gravel of the yard. "There," he said pointing at the weeds. "Those blue flowers, right there."

James was struck again by the thought that he had a lot to learn to live in this strange new world. He had to learn to live as his ancestors had lived. The technology that had been the foundation of all James had ever known was all either gone or going fast. His Grandpa cooking over an open fire was a perfect example.

As he ate the bacon and eggs that was the best breakfast he could remember having in a very long time, he asked Chuck why he didn't use the electric range in the kitchen. It seemed to James like the house had plenty of PV panels. As it turned out, the PV panels weren't the problem. Chuck's system didn't have enough battery capacity to always use the electric range. "Better to make sure the freezers keep working," Chuck told him. "Wish there was more of this bacon in there," he added. "We don't have any pigs, guess I wouldn't know how to make bacon, anyway. Got plenty of chickens, though. Don't guess we'll run out of eggs."

The freezers will stop, too, James thought. *None of it's going to work forever. Hell, even the solar panels won't work forever. Not only that,* he thought, *Grandpa's not going to be here forever, either.* He decided that he needed to learn as much from Chuck as he could about how to live without technology. He was sure Anna would be home soon, and he was starting to dream of having children and living here on the BR as his forefathers had done; without the aid of any modern technology.

"I sure am glad you're here, son," Chuck told him. "It's been a might lonely around here, waiting. Figured I was waiting and hoping for Anna to show up; didn't have much hope of seeing you or your mom again. Sure am glad I was wrong."

"Me too, Grandpa. Glad you waited. How long do you think it'll take Anna to get here?"

"Don't know, James. It's a damn long walk if she had to walk all the way." Chuck looked away from James, but not quick enough to hide the doubts that lay beyond the old man's dark brown eyes. "Guess now that you're here," Chuck changed the subject abruptly, "to help me, we should get that electric range out of the kitchen and put my great-grandmothers old wood cookstove in there. Always wondered why Dad kept that old antique stored out in the shop. Guess now I know."

It turned out that a lot of the old antiques that had been stored on the Blue River Ranch over the past hundred years would be worth much more than the modern marvels that had replaced them. From the draft horse harnesses, to the pedal-powered grinding wheel and blacksmith forge in the old shop, to the horse drawn implements that were weathering away in the scrap heaps behind it; Chuck and James filled the days with re-learning the old ways. Having grown up on the ranch and living there his entire life, it was much easier for Chuck than it was for James, but James learned more and more every day. The one constant to everything he learned was just how much physical hard work was involved. It was hard work from sunrise to sundown every single day. The days went by one after the other, and not a day went by that James didn't think this was the day that Anna would be home. The ranch truly did become home for James, as he started losing track of time.

They'd started putting up the hay crop from the mesa meadow just a couple of days after James' arrival. That had been interesting, to say the least. There hadn't been enough diesel left in Chuck's storage tank to complete the harvest using the modern implements, so they had to use a team of Belgian draft horses for part of the work. Chuck had always kept draft horses as a hobby, even using them to sometimes pull an old sled to feed cattle in the winter. To put up this year's crop of hay, Chuck had decided to do the cutting and raking with the horses, saving the diesel to power the tractor and baler. The cutting and raking worked out okay, after a lot of work in the shop getting the old horse-drawn sickle bar mower back into working condition; but the diesel ran out before they finished baling. It didn't take long for James to understand how much of an improvement baled hay had been to the old method of stacking using a horse-drawn buck rake and pitchforks. Bucking hay bales onto a wagon wasn't easy, but a lot more hay could be moved and stacked in a day than could be done the old-fashioned way. The baled hay was put into the hayloft of the log barn using an electric motor-powered hay elevator, but the loose hay they had to put up in stacks right in the field. The mechanism for lifting loose hay into the hayloft using a horse and ropes and pulleys was long gone. Chuck had commented that next year they would have to either rebuild a system to do that, or they would just have to not stack hay in the loft. Despite the hard work, James had really enjoyed learning how to harness up and work the draft horses.

Too much time had gone by with no sign of Anna. He had stopped counting days, but James was starting to drive himself crazy. He was finding it hard to concentrate, or even think about whatever task was at hand. His thoughts were constantly on Anna, wondering where she could be. He had tried not to even discuss it with Chuck anymore. He didn't want to hear any negative thoughts. Anna had to come home. She just had to. He kept thinking he should go look for her, but where? It was over a thousand miles from Kremmling to Eugene, and the multiple possible routes of travel made the odds of finding her incredibly slim.

"I have to go," he told Chuck. They were in the process of harvesting winter squash in the garden. "I need to go find Anna."

The statement caught Chuck by surprise. He set the two butternut squash gently down in the wheelbarrow. He wasn't surprised that James had been pining away for Anna. That wasn't a well-kept secret. He was surprised that his grandson would even be considering just heading out toward Oregon with about zero chance of ever finding anything, let alone Anna.

"How you gonna do that son? She might not even be alive," he tried to be as gentle as he could. "Pretty strong odds she didn't make it, you know."

"She did make it! I know it. She's out there…somewhere. She should have made it home by now."

"I hope she's alive, too, James." Chuck was as lonely as anyone. "But hope doesn't make it so. I wish your mother was still alive, and your grandmother. God, I miss Nancy." Chuck paused, trying to find the right words. "We just have to go on living as best we can James."

"You call this living?" the anger in James' voice stung the old man as much as his words. "What are we doing, Grandpa? Why are we just holed up here like we're the last people on earth? We aren't you know. You haven't even left the ranch, have you? Since, since it happened…"

There was pain in Chuck's voice as he answered, "Yes, yes I have left the ranch. After I buried the Durans, I rode over to the Crowley place and buried John and Martha. Then I went on down to Smith's and buried the whole family, all four of them." The memory of having to bury all of his neighbors was obviously hard on Chuck. He looked off into the distance. "I didn't go any farther, James. Guess I was just too tired of burying people."

James' anger and frustration gave way to pity. He couldn't be angry at Chuck, he felt as sorry for his grandpa as he did for himself. But this life was hardly worth living. This really wasn't living, at all; it was merely, and barely existing.

"We can't just go on like this, Grandpa," his voice was soft and even. "Life isn't worth living if this is all there is."

Chuck looked down at the ground and stroked his white beard in thought. The sorrow in his eyes was painful when he looked back up at James. "You're right, son. This isn't living. Tell you what, let's finish getting the squash into the cellar, and I'll ride into Kremmling with you tomorrow. Might be somebody there; somebody to give us a better idea of…of the odds."

It was obvious to James that Chuck didn't think Anna was alive. *She has to be,* he thought. *Grandpa's wrong. He has to be wrong. I'll find her. I won't stop at Kremmling. I'll keep going until I find her, or…or…*

James was up before dawn; truth was he'd hardly even slept. Hope and doubt had waged a war in his head all night long. He couldn't wait for daylight, *bound to be enough juice in the battery for just the kitchen light,* he thought. As quietly as he could, he got the fire going in the cook stove and got the pot of ground chicory started. By the time chicory finally started simmering, he figured he had enough heat to fry some eggs. *Eggs again.* James would never have believed he would ever get tired of eggs, but with the chickens laying more than two people could ever possibly eat, they ate more eggs than any other food.

Dawn was finding its way through the open kitchen windows by the time the six eggs were turning white in the old cast iron skillet. Chuck came into the kitchen wearing only his jeans and an old white undershirt. He went straight to the kitchen sink and washed his face and hands with cold water, not even bothering to use any of the warm water from the teapot that was always on the back of the stove.

"You okay, Grandpa?" James asked. Chuck seemed pale and he wasn't moving with his usual morning vigor.

"I'm fine son," he said, as he slumped into the chair at the end of the table. "That coffee ready?"

James poured a mug of the chicory coffee and set it on the table before flipping the eggs. He poured himself a cup while the eggs finished cooking, and gave each of them a plate of eggs before sitting down at the other end of the table. Chuck hardly moved. He held the coffee mug in one hand, with the mug and his elbow resting on the table. He was looking down at his eggs. Besides the pallid look of his skin, James thought his breathing wasn't quite right. He seemed to be taking slow deliberate breaths, as he stared at the plate of eggs. James couldn't tell if he'd even drank any of the coffee.

"Grandpa, you don't look so good. You sure you're okay?" What had been mild concern was turning to fear. What if his grandpa was really sick? What would he do?

Just as James was on the edge of panic, Chuck seemed to snap out of it. "I'm fine," he said, as he straightened up in his chair and took a sip of the chicory coffee. He set the mug back down and started chopping and stirring his eggs with his fork.

What a relief, James thought, as he dove into his own pile of eggs; morning hunger overcoming the monotony of the same old breakfast. James wolfed down his breakfast, getting more and more anxious to start out. He was still torn between the need to go find Anna and the fear that he never would. The fear that she was gone forever, that he would end up living here alone for his whole life gnawed at him. He fought that fear with hope. He had to believe. *She has to be alive,* he told himself. *She's out there, somewhere. She has to be. I'll find her alive, just like I found Grandpa.*

He looked up at his grandpa. Chuck was eating much slower than James. Slower even than normal. He seemed to be pushing eggs around on his plate more than putting them in his mouth. "Listen, Grandpa," James told him, as he got up and carried his plate over to the sink, "you don't have to go if you don't feel like it. Why don't you just stay here and rest? I'll ride into town and find out what I can. I promise I'll be back tonight." It would be a long hard day to ride all the way into Kremmling and back, but as much as he wanted to just strike out toward Oregon, he didn't want Chuck to have to make that ride if he was sick.

"I'm fine," Chuck told him, for at least the third time. "Go get our horses saddled up while I clean up breakfast. If we're going to ride all the way to town and back, we better get started."

James hesitated, but only for a moment. He was driven by a relentless hope, and equally as relentless fear that just wouldn't let go. Already dressed in his riding clothes, he headed out to the barn to saddle up Red and Midnight.

With the horses ready to go and tied up in the barn, James walked back toward the house. It seemed like Chuck should have been out by now. "Hey, Grandpa," he hollered from the mudroom on his way to the kitchen, "you ready to go?" He stepped through the kitchen door and froze.

Everything was almost the same as he'd left it. The chicory coffee pot was still steaming on the wood-burning stove, as was the large hot water tea kettle. Chuck's coffee mug sat on the table, still more than half full. His plate still had most of the pile of eggs drying in place, but the fork was laying upside down and sideways off to the edge of the table. Some egg had splattered out onto the table where the fork had fallen. Chuck wasn't exactly seated at the table. It looked like he'd dropped his fork and pushed himself back away from the table. But he never got up. He was slumped down in the chair, his hands dangling down below the arms of the chair that held him in place. His head was lolled forward with his chin resting on his chest; his dead eyes forever staring straight down. James' mind seized up. He stood there staring, knowing with certainty that his grandfather was dead, yet comprehending nothing. He was lost.

Chapter 17

The soft glow on the eastern horizon slowly brightens and the world suddenly springs to life, as the sun seems to leap over the peaks to the east. *Already quite a ways south,* he thinks, seeing the sunrise, and he wonders what day it is. James isn't even sure what month it is. *Must be October. Doesn't seem like October, I don't even need a jacket.*

James is sitting on the bench directly behind the headstones of the Pierson family cemetery. He has been sitting in that same spot since the sun dropped off the western edge of the world yesterday evening. He has to pee, but his body seems frozen in place. Standing and stretching only makes the necessity more urgent. He looks around as if someone might see him if he just opened his fly and pissed right here. *Wouldn't be respectful,* he thinks and walks over behind the three big Blue Spruce trees that his great grandfather planted behind the cemetery some seventy or eighty years ago.

What now? The thought seems strange. *His grave needs a cross. Why? Who's ever going to see it? I'm the only one left. Why me? What now?* He is back sitting on the bench in exactly the same place where he spent the night. He looks up from the earth that he finished mounding over the grave just before sunset last night. The sun has climbed a little way up the cloudless sky. That totally clear, deep blue sky that seems unique to the Rocky Mountains.

I should be hungry. It seems like a strange thought, even though he has had nothing to eat since yesterday morning.

Why should I eat? To live? He almost laughs. *They're all gone.* His eyes scan the markers of the final resting place of the sons and daughters of the Blue River Ranch. The markers vary from the old granite headstones of his great, great, great grandparents to the four simple wooden crosses where Chuck had buried the Duran family just six months ago. The four Duran family graves with their simple wooden crosses are arranged with a space between two sets of two crosses.

Grandpa left a spot for Anna, he thinks. *Mother should be buried here too. Not where I left her, back in Castle Pines. I should have brought her.* He thinks back to the journey from Castle Pines. *Could have been done, I could have brought her body.* He has a memory flash from childhood of one of Grandpa Chuck's favorite shows, **Lonesome Dove**. An image of the wrapped-up body of Gus McCrae draped over the back of a horse being carried back to the spot in Texas where he wanted to spend eternity.

What's the point? They're all dead. Dead is dead. I'm alive. Why? Why am I still alive? His eyes are a little blurred, but not crying, there is a kind of lump, almost a pain in his throat. He is barely conscious of the .357 revolver that he is holding in his lap.

Why not Julie? I loved Julie, why shouldn't she be here? She should be here, but you didn't bring her. Anna should be here, too. You loved Anna more than you ever loved Julie, but you ran out on her. You ran out on Anna, and you left

Julie to rot in that hell hole. At least I buried her with Mother. You should have buried them here with Grandpa.

He doesn't really even notice that he is raising the big revolver as he argues with himself. It's more like it moves of its own volition. He looks again at the space where Anna should be buried. *Who'll bury me?*

A movement catches his eye. There, down in the valley below, on the lane leading from old Highway 9 up to the ranch. At first, it doesn't register, then he realizes it's a horse. A horse with a rider coming up the lane toward the ranch. Too far away to tell for sure, the rider seems to have long black hair, it seems to be a woman. A lone rider coming up the road to the BR.

Looks like Anna. Can't be Anna, Anna's dead. Dead with the rest of them. But it looks like Anna. You must be hallucinating. But it looks like Anna. You know it can't be Anna, Anna's dead. The big revolver, which seems to move with a life of its own, as he argues with himself, stops and hovers, suspended in mid-flight, the end of the barrel just inches below his chin.

Somewhere high overhead, the chilling sound of an eagle's scream pierces the quiet stillness of the Colorado morning.

Author's Note:
If you enjoyed this story, please take a moment to review the book on Amazon. If you would like to contact me directly, please feel free to do so:
marcuslynndean@gmail.com
I welcome any and all feedback. Thank you,
Marcus Lynn Dean
May 2019

About The Author

After a lifetime of "personal" writing, **Marcus Lynn Dean** has finally found time in retirement to pursue his passions. He lives with his wife, Karen, in a scenic small community just outside of Cedaredge, Colorado.
The Scream Of An Eagle is his first novel. It is hoped that it won't be his last.
He is also the author of the controversial non-fiction work:
The Police States Of America, Whatever Happened To The Land Of The Free.

Made in the USA
San Bernardino, CA
18 June 2019